PRAISE FOR *100 BOYFRIENDS*

"Brontez Purnell's *100 Boyfriends* is a symphony of sex, trouble, and wisdom—as if the composer had sex with each member of the orchestra by way of getting it right. In this electric, prismatic, genre-defying punk literary flight, Purnell is twirling—I loved every page."

—Alexander Chee, author of *How to Write an Autobiographical Novel*

"Brontez Purnell has such seemingly casual genius that at times you forget you're reading a book and are transported to some couch/bus/basement where the drugs are really good and your friend is really funny, maybe your weird closeted cousin is on HarlemHookups in the corner, and all of a sudden your friend says some fucking Sappho-ass, weird-ass, brilliant-ass bullshit. I love this slut of a book, it's a slut-ass maker, *100 Boyfriends* or no new boyfriends at all, Purnell's autofiction / memoir / whatever the hell this marvelously sad and intoxicating book is shook me up good with its honesty and blunt-to-face endings, the jokes and stories I didn't know we were allowed to tell outside of circles of faggots and misfits. But this book is in those circles, makes you tea, and steals for you; it invites us in, but would we mind shutting the hell up 'cause it's a little hungover? The light is coming through the windows so clear."   —Danez Smith, author of *Homie*

"Each story in *100 Boyfriends* is a minor eclipse: stunning in scope, technically blinding, and entirely miraculous. I laughed and I cried and I laughed until I cried—Brontez Purnell is a marvel."   —Bryan Washington, author of *Memorial*

"In the vast history of the universe there is only one Brontez Purnell, and thank god we get him. From cruising to crushes, cumming to closure, *100 Boyfriends* is a mandatory read for the funny-sexy lit freaks among us—a candy box of Euro boys and Daddies, blue pills and satanic exes—all told in an addictively delicious voice by a writer who is somehow both wildly cool and self-deprecatingly humble at the same time." —Melissa Broder, author of *The Pisces*

"No one writes like Brontez Purnell. It's not just that he is hilariously irreverent, which he is, but that he reserves reverence for that which is deserving. *100 Boyfriends* is like a good lover, by turns vulgar and vulnerable, dirty and desperate, and always grinding toward magic." —Justin Torres, author of *We the Animals*

"Scathingly lucid, filthily pure, this is the most astute, witty, acid-tongued, and emotionally generous book about relationships—from one-night stands to internet no-no's to ill-conceived crushes to long-term loves, requited and otherwise—I've read. Painfully knowing yet never jaded, *100 Boyfriends* dissects, explodes, lambastes, and revels in the ugly beauty of imperfect intimacies with prose that consistently puts its finger on the bleeding pulse of contemporary desire. An unforgettable ode to the heart that beats inside every longing body." —Maryse Meijer, author of *The Seventh Mansion* and *Rag*

"The stories in *100 Boyfriends* took me on a journey: They made me laugh. They made me gasp. They made me feel. Brontez Purnell is a vibrant literary voice you won't soon forget. I love this book." —De'Shawn Charles Winslow, author of *In West Mills*

BRONTEZ PURNELL
100 BOYFRIENDS

Brontez Purnell is a writer, musician, dancer, filmmaker, and performance artist. He is the author of a graphic novel, a novella, a children's book, and the novel *Since I Laid My Burden Down*. The recipient of a 2010 Whiting Award for Fiction, he was named one of the thirty-two Black Male Writers for Our Time by *T: The New York Times Style Magazine* in 2018. Purnell is also the frontman for the band the Younger Lovers, the cofounder of the experimental dance group the Brontez Purnell Dance Company, the creator of the renowned cult zine *Fag School*, and the director of several short films, music videos, and, most recently, the documentary *Unstoppable Feat: The Dances of Ed Mock*. Born in Triana, Alabama, he has lived in Oakland, California, for more than a decade.

100 BOYFRIENDS

BOYFRIENDS

BRONTEZ PURNELL

MCD X FSG ORIGINALS

FARRAR,
STRAUS
AND
GIROUX
NEW
YORK

MCD × FSG Originals
Farrar, Straus and Giroux
120 Broadway, New York 10271

Library of Congress Cataloging-in-Publication Data
Names: Purnell, Brontez, author.
Title: 100 boyfriends / Brontez Purnell.
Other titles: One hundred boyfriends
Description: First edition. | New York : MCD x FSG Originals, 2021.
Identifiers: LCCN 2020042748 | ISBN 9780374538989 (paperback)
Subjects: LCSH: Gays. | Dating (Social customs)
Classification: LCC HQ76.25 .P87 2021 | DDC 306.76/6—dc23
LC record available at https://lccn.loc.gov/2020042748

Designed by Richard Oriolo

Our books may be purchased in bulk for promotional, educational, or
business use. Please contact your local bookseller or the Macmillan
Corporate and Premium Sales Department at 1-800-221-7945, extension
5442, or by email at MacmillanSpecialMarkets@macmillan.com.

www.fsgoriginals.com • www.fsgbooks.com
Follow us on Twitter, Facebook, and Instagram at @fsgoriginals

10   9   8   7   6   5   4   3   2

"Fuck all y'all"

CONTENTS

ACT I

ARMY OF
LOVERS

IN THE MORNING

I WOKE UP ALARMED. I didn't know where I was at first. It was that feeling of waking up someplace foreign and being like, "What the fuck?!" But then you look to the left and you're like, "Oh, wait, *that* handsome guy."

It's comforting to wake up with someone this attractive, and I'm sure he was thinking the same thing, but I also couldn't go back to sleep because his sun-spanked disco ball was flashing high beams all over the room.

His body was covered in them; even the cast on his leg was spotted with light.

Now, I had come in his room the afternoon before. His

roommate was having an after-kiki at their house. She was shit-faced and said, "Let's meet my roommate, y'all are probably gonna fuck."

We got high as fuck and covered every subject from nu jazz to childhood trauma.

I got in his bed and he motioned me closer and put me in a bear hug; I was taken aback because it had been a very long time since someone had touched me like this, let alone a really hot person in a cast.

"I'm going to leave you guys alone a second," my friend said, cocaine ring on her nose. He pulled me in tighter and I pulled off my glasses. His arms around me, I felt my dick get hard and went with the first action in my head.

"I should probably go now," I said.

"I'll be here all night," he said.

I made it home but—*Oh shit. I left my glasses.*

"Come back, please—now," he said when I called to see if they were there.

I was quickly back in his arms and this time he was on painkillers. He pushed my head down. I know for a fact that the night before, when I was in the midst of a cocaine and vodka-induced tirade, I explained that I don't like sucking dick. But I guess he changed my mind. I heard his voice. It was like an angel sighing. Or maybe like a dude on painkillers getting a blow job? All these vowel-dominant (though otherwise unintelligible) moaning sounds, punctuated with "yeah," "more," and "that feels good, dude." After half an hour or so, I left to attend a reading on the other side of town.

"Come back after?" he asked.

"Again?" I said, beginning to feel like someone actually needed me.

"Yes, again," he answered.

I went home and rinsed my ass out and then went to the reading and beelined to his door, to my knees, straddled over him.

"Get it in there," he said, followed by more vowel-dominant (yet otherwise unintelligible) moaning.

After he came, I dismounted and asked if he wanted to eat fried chicken. "Yes. Whiskey, too," he demanded.

Painkillers and whiskey—I liked his style.

"You're my boyfriend now—go get the food."

"I'm broke, and I don't feel like walking, plus it's cold outside and the fog just rolled in," I said, thinking that I had just successfully sidestepped my first duty as a fake boyfriend.

"Look in the closet, take the vintage blue Patagonia jacket—you can have it, in fact. My debit card is in my wallet. Take it, the PIN is five-six-nine-eight, then go to the basement and grab my bike. It's the chrome Bianchi Pista . . . and hurry the fuck up," he said, giggling.

I followed all his orders and was cruising down the street in his jacket, on his bike, with his money. I was gagged over the bike, as I am a vintage-bike junkie and Bianchi doesn't even make chrome Pistas anymore—I was gliding through the foggy nighttime feeling like the Silver Surfer, only on a bike.

The fried chicken place was a ten-minute ride away but first things first: How much money did this fool have in his checking account?

I stopped at the ATM and typed in his PIN, five-six-nine-eight, and pressed Balance: $80,690.78. Like wait, what the fuck?! After the transaction ended, I put the card back in the machine again and did it all over to make sure I had seen it right—and I had.

I pedaled onward to the restaurant, thinking in my head, *Like, what the fuck does that dude DO?*

A litany of questions sprang to mind. *Why does he live in that crappy room? Why does he live in that crappy apartment? If I stole twenty bucks from his account would he even notice or be bummed? Like, did he break his leg skiing in Tahoe or doing some other rich people shit?* And most importantly, *Should I try to marry him?*

I could not recall the last time my bank account or the bank account of anyone I knew closely held more than, say, four thousand bucks—and this was his checking, no less. What the fuck did his savings look like?

I quickly put it out of my head because thinking about money is gross and also the variables seemed too vast. You can't make any guesstimates about someone else's life without knowing them, and honestly I didn't know my fake boyfriend at all.

I biked past a storefront and caught a glimpse of myself in the reflection of the glass window. I looked like boyfriend material, or at the very least like some asshole who graduated from some WASP-ass college on the East Coast. But I knew I was an impostor underneath, which also turned me on because crime is sexy. But this was *his* expensive vintage Patagonia, *his* expensive vintage Bianchi, and *his* debit card. Dear god, was this how he felt every day? Like a capable, normal adult?

The woman at the restaurant who took my order asked for my ID when I presented his debit card, and I said, cool as a cucumber, "Oh, it's not my card, it's my boyfriend's, he broke his leg and I have to do, like, everything for him now." She didn't even blink before she let me sign the check. Did she notice how much I was glowing inside when I said "my boyfriend"? Fake or not, something about saying "my boyfriend" just felt good.

I biked the food back to his apartment.

I did not steal twenty dollars from his well-endowed-ass bank account.

I made it back to his house and soon after, the night got blurry. Morning was crisp yet hungover.

I had stared at him so long he actually opened his eyes; about three beats later I asked, "Does this mean we're boyfriends now?"

"Yes, exactly," he said, cracking the fuck up.

I kissed him on the lips and got dressed quickly so that I could be late for work.

"I like boys that are broken like you—you're dependent and can't get away," I teased.

He rolled his eyes, like, so hard. "What are you gonna do when my leg heals?"

"Fuck if I know, break it again?" I said, trying to hold a straight face.

Just then, whatever bastard cloud that was covering the sun lifted, and light shined through the window brighter than before. It hit the disco ball, and bright specks of light were everywhere again.

There was the superstitious part of me that wanted to take it as a sign—*This guy, this guy will be my new boyfriend*—but immediately something in my head said, *Probably not*.

I went with my second instinct and turned to leave.

"I'll be here all day. Will you come back to me, please?" he asked, looking me dead in the eye.

"Yes. I'll come back whenever you want me to," I said, and left.

HOOKER BOYS
(PART ONE)

I

My writer's block had kicked my ass something terrible and I couldn't break out of it. I watched each and every night disappear from under me in limitless fountains of vodka. One afternoon it felt like thunder had struck me.

Vitamin C . . . I need a liter, I said to myself.

I had woken up destroyed and feeling the sunlight. It was brutal, like nature was reminding me that I was a bad person. Truth told I wasn't a bad person—I was just hungover. These feelings come up sometimes.

Now, I admittedly was in a bad way. It was noticeable.

Friends were having conversations about it. I had lost jobs. The only redeeming aspect was that most of my friends were as fallible as I was so I endured no menacing judgment, but I *felt* it. I knew it was happening without someone having to say it to me. My inner compass was at a very loud volume.

Some friends had died and some were disappearing, having babies and going away, getting old and weary and going away, or simply going crazy in secret and going away—it all had the same effect. The climate felt colder.

I, being sober for the first time in six hours, was feeling anxious. I needed relief. I wanted a hooker.

I was still technically a handsome man—or, rather, my mother often told me I was handsome—but I wanted more control. I wanted to pay someone for a specific experience at a specific time and after we were done we would specifically know it was over. I wanted a hooker.

I knew him from years before; he lived in Los Angeles now. He was Hollywood handsome yet not out of reach. He was on TV, he campaigned for Black Rights, and he also dressed like a hooker from outer space.

"How much?" I texted.

"Well, for you, just 'cause you're you, 200 bucks," he texted back.

He came over in a leather jacket and cheetah-print bike shorts. I, though being what I considered a "groovy" person, winced a little. I wanted him to come over in straight-boy drag like I knew he did with all his other clients. I wanted him to pretend that his name was, like, Chad or Jonah, but instead he came in and looked at me with these warm eyes, a look that said, "I know I'm being paid to have sex with a friend."

His doggy-style game was so on point; his dick and technique were also of note, like, you could tell he fucked for a living. I bottomed like a porno bottom to impress him; I tried to impress him to the point where I was like, "Wait—I'm paying *him*, shouldn't he be impressing *me*?"

I came three times.

I rolled over on the bed and looked him in the eye. It was that deep, weird, "You're really pretty" look, like you're looking at something both far away and right in front of you. He picked up on it.

"You want a drink really bad, huh? I can tell," he said.

"The world is a lot clearer with alcohol," I said. We both laughed, though the statement hit a bit closer to home than I wanted it to.

We started kissing again.

I asked him kindly not to tell any of our mutual friends that this had happened. I also asked if this would warp our friendship, like, from here on out to eternity would I have to pay him, or could there be a random tryst thrown in every once in a while?

"Sure," he said, though I couldn't quite distinguish which part of the question he was saying "sure" to.

2

Mike was the first hooker R.J. had ever lived with. They were both nineteen and living in this warehouse in the Tenderloin. Various factors had brought both boys there, a dizzying mix of a general lust for adventure and troubled homelives that needed to be escaped from, and where else would one live in San Francisco for five hundred bucks? It was 2002 and both of their times had come to go big, make mistakes, and attempt adulthood.

Mike was gay as fuck but for some reason was dating this girl who he lived with in a single-room occupancy in the warehouse. R.J. suspected the love was fueled by a mutual passion for methamphetamines, and he was right. Mike and R.J. were sharing their usual cup of stale coffee and splitting a croissant when Mike explained how the girl, Lisa, paid the rent and how he turned tricks to buy both of them speed. "It works out perfectly," said Mike, and he hurried R.J. along out of the café and on to their next appointment.

R.J. had a profound respect for Mike; though they were the same age, Mike was way older in his heart. R.J. had just moved to San Francisco from some sleepy nowhere place in New England without prior access to things like drugs and sexual danger. He would walk through the city, and even on quiet days, his heart would pound with excitement.

Anything could happen here, he would often say to himself.

Mike had grown up just outside the city without much parental nagging about his whereabouts or activities. He had been whoring his way through S.F. since his early adolescence and was now bestowing his knowledge on his newfound brother R.J. That very morning, for instance, Mike instructed R.J. to not wear those short shorts with his ass and front pockets hanging out.

"You have to dress like a boy, otherwise we won't get money," Mike said, rubbing an obscene amount of Old Spice deodorant under his armpits.

The two had been walking through the Tenderloin asking any man who looked older than thirty for spare change and bus transfers. Mike was good at talking to people and getting things he wanted from them. R.J. let Mike do all the talking. They had some five bucks in change now and Mike explained to R.J., "You know what I like? Change! And, like, if I'm gonna have change, I want *radical* change, like, for everything to just do a hundred-eighty-degree turn all at once. It's more exciting that way."

R.J. took everything Mike said as the honest-to-god truth, perhaps for no other reason than that he sounded convinced of it. He also marveled at how the gears in Mike's head turned; his thoughts were what he imagined spark plugs to fire off like—that statement about the radical change business hadn't been preceded by anything except a long silence.

"We're here," said Mike, and the two made an abrupt stop.

They had walked to one of the many secret porn studios south of Market. Mike had done some film work before and had caught wind of an ad in the back of the paper looking for bottoms to get fucked by this automated robotic dildo contraption called "The Butt Machine." R.J. hadn't bottomed a day in his life and the machine looked like the scariest fucking thing he had ever laid eyes on.

The director who let them in led them down a hall past what looked to be a mock prison cell with chains attached to the walls. "You only have to get fucked by the machine for twenty minutes and you make a hundred and thirty-five dollars and we put it on the webcam. Can you boys get undressed?"

They both took their clothes off and ten seconds later the director ordered them to put them back on.

"You, call me back," said the director, and handed his card to Mike.

The two boys walked back to the warehouse where they lived together for about another six months, until Mike had a breakdown on speed and had to move away.

Some years afterward, R.J. spotted Mike on the train, dressed very normal with two other normal gentlemen.

R.J. proceeded to greet Mike. Mike hugged him, kissed him, stared deep into his eyes, and asked, "Sorry, it's been so long, what's your name again?"

3

He was a handsome older Black man. He had been some form of professional back in the eighties and nineties and had been retired for many, many years—that's what he told me.

He always made me meet him in the study part of his loft

apartment. There were books, like, soooooo many books. Art on the wall and a desk with a computer and one black leather love seat, the one I always had to kneel down in front of and suck his dick while he was sitting naked in it. "You are the prettiest boy I've ever had. Be good to Daddy," he said. I was twenty but I got the feeling he said this to all the boys. It still felt good to hear.

I was hooking 'cause all the other boys I knew were doing it too. I felt like I had to prove to them I could do it. Back when it was legal I put an ad in the back of the gay Castro newspaper that said "best blow job at a reasonable price." He was my first repeat customer.

The first time we met I was on my knees sucking him off and he saw the tattoo of a woman's name on my chest. He asked, "Is that your girlfriend?"

"No," I replied, "it's my mother." His body visibly convulsed and he jizzed all over my tattoo. I was too young to know that I should have not made him a repeat customer.

His body was round and smooth and warm. He would hold me after sometimes, and all the other boys told me I should charge more but I didn't. He felt too good. Or maybe the attention felt good. I would let him have his way. I would feel the soft caress of a hand that pulled me away from control, and I was too young to know that all men who want to extract something from you generally have the sweetest touch. "You are the prettiest boy . . ." He said it so much I began to internalize it.

I only charged fifty dollars for sessions that were supposed to be just a blow job and last an hour but instead would turn into much, much more and would go on until the sun came up.

He had a wife and kids at some point; I surmised that much. There were older pictures of him hugging a woman and two young boys all over the apartment—in the hallway and the living room: besides the bathroom and study, the only parts of the house I was allowed to hang out in. My suspicions were confirmed when he finally said, "You know, I have sons about your age."

When I came over, though, he always led me to the study. I just knew that if I sucked his dick enough times in one month (he would call me over four times a month—only on the weekends) I would have enough money for weed or the new pair of Jordans I wanted. I loved him—or at least I thought that this was what love felt like.

One time after I blew him he lit a cigarette and said, "You are not like the other boys—you like to stay with Daddy." He was right.

One weekend he took me on a hike. On the trail he pounced and ripped my pants and underwear down. He took me in the middle of the hiking trail and I felt embarrassed, like someone would walk along the trail and see.

But I couldn't say no to him. It excited me to get fucked on a trail with nature. It was like I was this special thing. I knew in the long run it would not last.

I saw him in public one day walking with two young men close to my age. I had a feeling they were his sons. As I inched closer to them on the sidewalk his eyes met mine and he shook his head at me, as if to say, "No—not here, not now." I wanted to be hurt but the fact was that that man was a stranger and not my real father. I would soon know all the ways in which men were not to be depended on. I walked away that day.

The years crept by and so did we—his dick stopped working and I grew from hooker to waiter to college graduate. I didn't really need to fuck for money anymore and I left it to the young boys.

I remember the last time he saw me and how shocked he was that my hair was beginning to gray. We lost touch, of course, but whenever I think of him I am always reminded of how pretty I am.

INHERITED
WINTER COAT

MY FATHER KILLED A MAN ONCE. It was an accident.

He was driving a train between Tennessee and Alabama and saw a young man stand on the tracks and freeze in place—he wanted to commit suicide, it seemed.

My father said he screamed and screamed, but it takes a full two miles to stop a train. He saw the boy explode on impact, torso torn from limbs. He also said that he saw the boy's eyes before the train hit him—that was the part he could never forget, the part he still saw even when he closed his own eyes.

I was having a similar feeling of internal combustion, albeit a less violent one; I was hungover and riding in a car along the Tennessee and Alabama state line and saw a train speeding alongside for a stretch and again thought about my father, who was now gone himself. He had died unexpectedly months before and I was still in mourning—sometimes the pain would dry up suddenly, and sometimes it would fall down all around me like rain. I was currently in a dry period.

I was riding down to my grandmother's house to rescue a peculiar inheritance: some guns of my father's, and some of his winter coats.

Driving the car was the man I loved. He decided to go with me—he wanted to be there for no other reason than to be a shoulder to lean on. He said he knew there would be tears.

I had forgotten about the Appalachian foothills, the rolling blankets of trees and hills that covered the landscape with green, gold, auburn, or white, depending on the season. I'd been in California too long and forgotten about seasons, these dramatic stages—oppressive humid summers, sudden blizzards in the winter, flash floods or tornadoes. I had no internal sense of season anymore and had as of late been ignoring my own personal seasons. My life in the California sunshine was coming to an end—I felt it. I sat quietly, often, and waited for instinct to guide me to the next thing, whatever it was.

I forgot how the mountains here bled water. Whole jutting waterfalls just shooting out of the rocks like a shower hose. I was having my own eruption of emotion.

My lover was driving. The night before, I held him close in bed and was beside him and beside myself. Why did this feel so good? My sex life was absurd. Typically I crawled through bathhouses and felt swept aside; the sex with him wasn't lustful or "manly" or full of unspoken rage. It was this thing that I hadn't had in a long time. It was closer to comfort. Like, I really was right there next to him—I was THERE. Is this what love felt like?

Back to our mission. My father had a bunker on my grandma's land in southern Alabama. A collection of modera vintage winter coats and a collection of antique rifles, one with the name "Jody" engraved on it. The name of my great-great-grandfather. We were going to go to my grandma's land, pick up the coats and rifles, go down to New Orleans for two days, and come back up to lover boy's house in Tennessee. I would fly back to California from there. I figured if we were smuggling guns across that many state lines I should let a white boy drive—they're good like that.

I remembered my father—he was an OG. His coat collection was one of his prized achievements; even I as his only son could not outrank it. I asked once when I was a boy, "Die-dee"—as I pronounced his name—"can I have your coat?" He was wearing this tan-and-green houndstooth number with wooden buttons and a large collar on it; it was long, almost to his knees. His older brother had been a mod and played in soul bands in the seventies—he had stolen his style from him.

"You can't fit in Dad's coat yet, son. You can have it when I die." I couldn't have been more than eight when he said it.

He said it in a way where I knew he never intended to die. I thought about this memory as we pulled into a rest stop off the highway, and I almost cried but caught myself.

"Hey, baby—can we stop at Popeyes?"

"Yes, sir," said my handsome driver.

I had done this drive to my grandma's all through my youth. My father would drive four hours north to get me for Christmas and summer break, and I would sit and follow the roadway markers with my eyes and just feel content. Lover boy and I stopped in Birmingham, where we found a Popeyes, and, another hour and a half south, we found ourselves close.

The way to my grandma's was the same as I remembered. It was all Gulf Coastal Plain Spanish moss, two-lane highways, dirt roads, and Reconstruction-era decay. Everything—even the sparse houses that were obviously lived-in—all seemed eerily vacant. I was vacant.

My grandmother was from Gee's Bend; at some point in history a bunch of super scared white people burned a ferry so Black people couldn't travel to vote there. This is as much as I remembered of what my family had told me. My boyfriend was white as fuck, and he was probably (besides insurance sales-men) one of only a dozen or so white men who had set foot in this stretch of land in twenty years.

There were so many abandoned churches. We parked and explored one a mile before my grandma's house. It was dilap-idated. I remembered my father driving me to my grandma's house on the dirt roads of Wilcox County, where there were always cars parked on Sundays. We went in. The pews were stripped bare, there was mold everywhere, holes in the floor, wood planks strewn about the floor, and holes in the ceiling. How had it disintegrated so fast? It had been nine years since I saw it last. It seemed like that was too fast for something like that to just . . . all but disappear.

My mother had explained to me that buildings needed human breath in them to keep them moist and held together. Abandoned buildings are like abandoned people—they die sooner.

We explored it. Lover boy had a vintage camera from the sixties and there was just enough light in the abandoned church to take photos. I was staring at him and was a bit stuck. His camera was pointed directly at me.

What's his name again? I thought. I sat silent for a full twenty seconds. *Trevor, TREVOR, Trevor, his name is Trevor . . . phew!*

He told me to stand in front of a stained-glass window that had a hole busted in the top of it. He liked the shattered rainbow light it was casting—it would not matter ultimately because the photo would be in black and white. But I obliged because I understood he wanted to get the feeling right.

He took the picture and I got fearful because the floor was weak in places, so I asked him if we could leave.

We made it to my grandmother's house and got out of

the car and walked past the backyard about some half mile through the deep woods. We stopped at a clearing my father had made to hunt deer, and under the watchtower he had built in this tree was a bunker unit that was locked up. My aunt had mailed me the key to it some weeks before. We opened it and stepped in. The bunker wasn't bigger than a toolshed but it was neatly organized.

There was no electricity but there was enough sun to make out everything. His rifles were hung at the back of the shed on holders he had nailed to the wall. There were five in all, including the one from the twenties with my great-great-granddad's name engraved on the wood. I ran my hands across it. "Jody"—it looked shabbier than I remembered as a kid, and, perhaps a little too overcome with emotion, I kissed it.

I saw under a table to my right the old army chest my dad had in his military days in his late teens. I knew the coats were there. I just knew.

I opened it and I saw, sitting on top of the stack, the tan-and-green houndstooth coat. He put it in last, as if he knew I was the one who was going to find it. It was still in excellent condition—he had taken great care with it. This time, before I could get overly emotional, I heard Trevor calling from the door.

"Baby, let's come back here on our way from New Orleans. We should hit the road because it's getting dark soon and I want to get off these two-lane highways," he said matter-of-factly. I began to move. I grabbed an old hunting backpack my father had and put three coats in it. We carried four rifles and vowed to get the other stuff on the trip back.

We cut across the bridge leading to the main highway and I decided I missed California and that I would never come back to this place again. Another thirty minutes down the road Trevor asked to marry me. I said yes.

THE BOYFRIENDS

Boyfriend 007 / The Waiter

He had murdered a boy for me once. Knocked that faggot right the fuck out. We were in our twenties and Samuel Myers (that ASSHOLE) made a rude comment about my body. My knight in shining armor ignored his years of good breeding and waiter etiquette (did I mention this all went down in the twenty-four-hour diner hellhole we worked in together?), ripped off his apron, and socked that asshole Samuel Myers in the face. I owed him—that Valentine's Day I put a fifty-dollar bill in his tip jar with a note that said YOU MURDERED A BOY FOR ME ❤.

Boyfriend 99.5(%) / The Dreamer

He explained to me (and he was VERY drunk), "I've never wanted to be a star in the sky. They all die anyway and I'm too vain for death. I'm ether, or whatever you call it. That negative blank space the stars float around in. Olbers' paradox at play, you could say. The place that was there before the stars and will be there long after. Untouchable but you're surrounded by it. It's quicksand, I guess. I can explain more . . . Have you ever noticed how things in life always wanna leave you? Men will leave you, your looks will leave you (this is why I often practice looking like hell), your money will leave you. This is all fine. BUT. Something you build with your own two hands, that is (sometimes) always yours to keep. Let's say you write a book. Let's say the book is so good it outlives you, its toughest critics, and also several generations of people unaware of its existence. Maybe what I'm asking is unanswerable, but it gets back to that first feeling I was talking about—like, your immortal-ass book and the words within it are just floating forever on the page, sailing on this forever, just like a certain terrain Diddy Bopping all along the same kind of sea. Untouchable, unreachable, yet, it's everywhere, there's a 'there, there'—can you imagine?" He smiled, but I was already asleep.

Boyfriend Zero / The Fashion Editor

The silence was deafening but that wasn't the only cliché present in the room. The man hadn't changed his make-out music

since the nineties—it was all Cibo Matto tapes and other arti-
facts from his old hipsterdom that he carried around like duf-
fel bags. The time they spent together felt like it was always in
between sunsets; the red-orange final glow of the final minute
of the day had not quite mixed in with the new purple of night.
The sex was stuck within that same standstill. "I don't feel like
it tonight," they both said at the same time, and giggled upon
doing so. With no other reason to oppose each other, and nothing really to prove, they hopped into bed and held each other
even after their skin pressed together and the bed got uncomfortable and sweaty, but neither of them bothered to change
the sheets because it just didn't feel that serious.

Boyfriend #77 / The Chef

He invited me to his headquarters. He cooked for the Kings
and Queens of Art, making expensive vegan shit inspired by
nineties rock musicians. He explained to me what my feelings
were, often. Oh my god, he was everything I couldn't have but
the second I did have him I knew I didn't want it anymore. It
was like wanting a shot of whiskey and letting it sit on the bar
in front of you for entire minutes, mouthwatering. It wasn't
about the whiskey per se but more about letting the anticipa-
tion build. Sooner rather than later I was knocking back shots
of him like a fucking prizefighter.

Boyfriend 2.0 / The Firefighter

He said he wanted to set me on fire like a cigarette—he inhaled me with vigor, indulgence, and did so really, really carelessly. I was part of a pack, you see, or by knowing him I was in a carton, and most mornings seemed the same to him no matter who was there the night before. I don't think the boys meant much to him. His chain-smoking seemed in unison (disunion?) with the other facts. He was a firefighter, a big strong one. He had muscles from the time he was barely a teenager. He showed me video clips of him skateboarding on a suburban Southern California cul-de-sac, it had made his body strong and blessed with that lean, cut muscle pattern, probably how he got so fucking cocky. I met him years ago—I was living in a warehouse near downtown. He would follow me up to my room like a puppy and it would happen: semen flying everywhere. He was way taller than me so I fit neatly into him after the squirting epic semen battle we would have. He went away at some point, lived up in the Northern California woods. He was the one who kept rural California from turning into a chuck of ashes.

He had just finished fighting a stint of fires in Mendocino. He got naked. I could see the places where the backpack equipment was irritating his skin. But he still had it. "Sorry I didn't give you any dick last time I was in town," he said. (We had never really fuuuuuuuucked before.) But this time, this was the test. It all felt—and heaven help me for saying this—"sweet," like we had waited. He was the only man I knew whose sex was that fluid: boy, girl, everyone in between, whichever race, that boy was sticking his dick in everybody and I admired the caliber of slut he was. He showed me pictures of his baby daughter and we read to each other all afternoon. He left after that for good.

Boyfriend #33 / The Hairdresser

I needed asymmetry, so I wanted to bleach my hair from side to side. I was disconnected from this one (spark) plug I needed to fully realize the projection. I was a filmmaker, I was about to finally find it and dream big and lucidly. What could not be imagined? Nothing, I decided. I started on my hair—it was still nonbleached. My hairdresser was sexy. Chubby angel face with a chubby angel dick. I noticed one time that his hands were cracked and calloused from all the chemicals, and the colorings, and the sewing weaves in till 2:00 a.m., as he had the only shop that took walk-ins past ten. He would sometimes take people as late as 1:00 a.m., and for a Black woman's hair salon, goddammit, that was of note. But he was fast, could sew in a weave in like forty-five minutes flat (I saw him do it once). I watched on the movie screen in my head, from my throne of the director's chair (but really, I was in his salon seat), as he slapped purple goop across my head. The chemicals sat so long I started to feel dizzy. "The longer you keep it on, the blonder it will be," he said. I didn't come to wuss out—I came to be blond, goddammit. I sweated it out. He conditioned my head and we fucked in the back of the shop. He filmed it. The next day my hair turned the color and texture of cotton candy and all fell out.

Boyfriend #40 / The Gentleman

They were the weirdest couple I had ever fucked. They made me slightly uncomfortable. They drank wine and fought a lot but did it in a way where you could tell deep, deep down they literally hated each other. One boyfriend was this white top who had a big-ass dick, and thank god he was hung because he was dumb as fuck. He didn't know what calculus was. He had a deep-ass country accent and was telling us a story about how he had woken up in a jail cell covered in feces one night and he almost went to jail for longer but luckily his mother loaned him $12,000 and it all got cleared up. His boyfriend was this Mexican artist boy who kept eyeballing me like he wanted to cut me because I was fucking his white-ass boyfriend. The top got drunker and had to go to bed and it was late so I stayed over and slept on the couch. In the middle of the night the Mexican boyfriend woke me up because he wanted to fuck, and I couldn't get my clothes off fast enough. He came and then stood over me. I could feel the inside of my butthole, that wet squishy thick feeling, like he had left factual evidence that he had been there. He politely started folding my clothes and setting them beside me. He kissed me on the forehead and very passionately on the lips and then he whispered, "You have to go now."

DAMN A LOVER
COMES HOME TO DIE

HE SHOWS UP TO MY HOUSE unannounced again—he's fresh
off a however-many-day speed binge. His shoes are missing.
He's panting hard and he smells like he's been walking bare-
foot in the hot streets for miles.

My heart sinks deep. He's different from the European
cologne–wearing, fragrant dandy I once knew him to be; he
had bewitched me from the first day I laid eyes on him. It was
with little effort on his part, I knew this much—his wish was
my command, even when he had nothing to say. He was never
the boy who everyone could love. He was kind of an asshole,

but more importantly he was something that God had tailor-made just for me.

He was funny, morbidly beautiful, always horny, and if it wasn't so sad there might have been something about his self-destruction that seemed sexy. Perhaps it was sexy when we were younger—it had morphed from sexy to demonic long ago. Yet he still had that power over me, this thing that I could never explain, like saying no to him was always out of the question.

Even in the half a second it took for all these thoughts to flash and materialize in my mind, I sense that he's already annoyed at the slow recognition in my eyes. Like he's daring me not to let him in.

He says nothing, and I'm taken aback, because the first time this happened it was an explosion—this is the second time he's come over strung out and I tell myself it will be the last but I also said that last time and now I'm not so sure.

THE FIRST TIME, he was crazed and out of his mind. It was a very active disassociation. He was convulsing and dry heaving. He started breaking things and yelling at me, telling me to get the fuck out of his apartment, that he would kill me. The situation was moving so fast that I stood there silent and still. He took off his shirt and pants and the track marks on his arms and legs looked like a constellation of stars. He lay on the couch but as soon as he lay down he popped back up; he ran out of my apartment in his underwear and I ran after him, chased him down the street, shouted for him to come back, but he just ran faster and faster. This was some years ago. I just assumed that he would be dead soon, and tucked the memory away.

This time he is quieter. There isn't any energy left in him and he's so thin I want to cry. I shave his head and make him a bath and throw away his smelly, mangled clothes. I go look for clean things I have for him so that he can lie in bed with me later. I turn the air conditioner on because I know he is burning up and he likes his pillow and sheets cold when his body settles into bed. I remember that much from when we lived together.

It had been his apartment first, some fifteen years before. These days people talk about how expensive the city is but dear god, even when a one-bedroom apartment was $650 a month we basically couldn't afford it. I got kicked out of my spot and he let me move in because he wanted me close. He wanted to play house. It just worked. Or rather it worked for longer than I thought it would.

This boy, as far as he and I are concerned, could show up to my house with a severed head and I would still let him in—that's how unnecessarily devoted to him I am. I remember saying to him in our youth, "No, I'll never leave"—he held me to my words like a steel trap stabs into a bear.

I run a bath for him and put him in. The boy who I actually missed is long, long gone. But I cannot sever myself from what remains. What was once a big beautiful star has collapsed in on its own weight and turned into a black hole.

. . .

I REMEMBER WHEN we were younger—he was the one who picked me. I remember it. I worked as a waiter at the diner near this spot he bartended at. We couldn't have been more than twenty-two at the time. He would come after his shift at the bar and I remember he came in for a week in a row at 3:00 a.m. He would sit in the same place and stare at me—I'd ask him, "Is there something I can get you, sir?" And he would always say with kind eyes, "No, you're fine," and nurse his cup of coffee another thirty or so minutes. I would see him eyeing my every move and I always found it rude. He explained to me after I moved in with him that he wasn't trying to be, and said, "I don't think I had ever seen anything like you before," and to the present day he had never really clarified that statement. Anything like me how? Did he mean a punk boy who worked at a diner? Dear god, at the time the whole city was CRAWLING with the likes of me. Or did he mean a Black boy like me? Or did he mean something outside the Venn diagram of sociopolitical identity politics?

I can only imagine he meant Black because though he loved me I know that he did not see us as the same thing. I knew that I read as "other" to him, and I learned why one day.

To the eye he looked like some Mission cholo dude—or at least that's where one's sexual desire would go when meeting him. He was Mexican, 6'3", bigger built, face of a fallen-ass angel (there were tattoos all over it), and he just had the style. Graffitied skateboard and a black hoodie and a Giants cap. He had a gold crucifix necklace that I liked to mentally fixate on whenever he wore it, which basically was every day. I had fucked enough boys with Catholic damage to know that if he's wearing a crucifix, he's definitely a ho. That boy was a ho. Yet still, that shit was all a crafted look 'cause his ass was as Orange County as a strip mall next to Disneyland.

I remember the first holiday that he dragged me to Southern California to meet his folks. I expected some charged, colonially Spanish feast of tamales or mole, but his family home had a framed American flag in the living room and I think I offended his mother when I looked visibly taken aback when they served a TV dinner for Thanksgiving. They had the TV on the entire time playing the news. It felt like I was in some form of hell and it made me feel a certain way for him. How on Earth did he grow up in *this*?

I remember him saying to me once, "I just like that you're *from somewhere*—I don't feel like I'm *from somewhere*." I remembered the scene from Thanksgiving and understood what he meant. But this was one of the many holes he had in himself that he always made visible to me.

I never really needed to stare deep into some crystal ball to understand what his issue was. He had this way of always laying the problem out as plainly as possible.

Like how I was living with him in his house but he had boyfriends—a great many Daddies and some other boys our age. Sometimes I had to meet them and it was always the same. Some weird person who existed out of the realm of our life; he was always trying to "date up." None of these men ever stayed for long and I found it rude as fuck that he even had the nerve to flaunt his whores in front of me.

Either way he chose me as his pet and for a long time we were happy. We were happy for longer than I thought we would be.

Our encounters blossomed into nights of us roaming the town high as fuck, well into the dawn. He would show up to my diner with bags of whatever drugs he copped at his bar and we would snort them and wait till 6:00 a.m. for my graveyard shift to end before heading to this one bar that was open all day, and we would party into the afternoon. We did this on a loop of what seems like years but in reality could maybe have been months. Time with him always seemed queered and distorted. A day with him seemed like both an hour and a lifetime. That's the type of love we had.

I remember one night we got drunk and got into a fistfight about nothing at a bar and got kicked out. We found a store-front several blocks later and made up—we started kissing on the ground and then I remember we had sex on the sidewalk, three different people walked past us and didn't even stop to notice. God bless San Francisco.

Another night he was so drunk he said that if I truly loved him I would do anything he said, and I responded, "Yes. I love you. I will do anything you say." And so he grabbed me by the arm and we ran under an 18-wheeler stopped at a red light and made out underneath it for what seemed like forever until we heard the gears shift and sprinted from beneath it before it ran us over.

There were rules, of course—he never called me his boyfriend. We fucked, we lived together, we almost died together partying, all that shit. But he was the lover and I was the beloved. I was to obey what he said; it was like this incestuous brotherhood where I was the younger one who was to take every cue from him, which was a strange arrangement considering we were the same age.

My relationship to him was always a very specific kind of mindfuck—behaving as boyfriends when we weren't but actually were. We did all the things two people who know each other too well do. We took turns being bored a lot. Whenever I was present, physically or mentally, he wasn't—even when we were at the same table eating or in the same bed fucking.

IT HAPPENED THAT he just stopped coming home. He was always into the older Daddies, the ones who led him down darker paths than he had planned for me. He would brag about this one Daddy who had leather blackout curtains, and how he would sit and do drugs with him for days and not see the sunlight. I got tired of cleaning him up after his binges. I always felt like the Daddies he chased got to burn all the good parts of him up with the drugs they pumped into him, like they all wanted to turn him into some drugged-up porno pup. When they were done with him I would always have to glue the pieces back together. Somewhere in the back of my head—despite all factors making it seemingly unfathomable—I thought that he would ask me to marry him. I learned that the most I would ever be was his nurse and his surrogate boyfriend. If he hadn't rescued me all those years ago from homelessness I probably could break the spell he has over me, but his early generosity has me locked in this position like a seat belt. I was on this ride, and on this ride, I would stay. We're both thirty-two now.

I remember when his absence from the apartment became permanent. I didn't hear from him and he stopped paying rent. I feared he was dead until that first time he came knocking on the door. He saw the apartment we once shared together and all he saw was me moving on with my life without him, and I guess it set him off. I didn't understand why he chose to ignore the fact that he was the one who abandoned me.

I PUT HIM IN $130 white Champion sweatpants I just got at the store when I recently went on a shopping spree high on pills; I pair them with the matching $130 white hoodie because I want to wrap him in expensive things and get him to my comfortable bed.

I trace his body with my eyes and I know he cannot sleep. The drugs are hammering through him like a freight train. I know his body like it's my own, and along his torso are a ridiculous bunch of pro-American, Sailor Jerry–style tattoos, spread all across his chest and belly, but from the start of his left clavicle and going up you can see where his tattoos had moved into weirder Aztec imagery. He started that phase when he moved to San Francisco and became more "woke." He had an outline of some Aztec warrior god along his clavicle and neck, and I remember the line work of the god's hand sits perfectly on top of the part of his neck where his jugular vein would pump bloody murder whenever he was high. I would sometimes just watch it move up and down and up and down and damn near hypnotize myself.

I get a bucket of ice water and sit it by the bed with a rag in it. I keep the lamp on the nightstand on and stay up with him. Every time I wipe his head with cold water I say, "You are going to behave yourself. You are going to come back to me."

BOYFRIEND #666 /
THE SATANIST

I HAD OUT-TROLLED MYSELF ONCE AGAIN. I wanted Trench Coat Mafia dick so I started putting out dating ads looking for adult players of Magic: The Gathering and Dungeons & Dragons—I was curious to see what would come from the net I had cast, and the answer would be standing in front of me sooner rather than later. I got a late-night text from a gentleman caller who said he was a ninth-level warlock and that he could teach me both the fantasy games and blow my back out. I got to his house and was literally so not prepared—like, I thought I was, but that fool was on his ninth-level warlock swag, SOOOO HARD. Before me stood a grown-ass man with surgically implanted fangs, a cape, red contact lenses, and an inverted pentagram tattoo on his forehead. The tattoo distracted from his gentle features; he really was a pretty guy, though he fucked in this ugly way. He asked me about my own inverted pentagram tattoo and I was like, "Oh, well, really I'm a Romantic Satanist—I believe in Satan as an allegory and as a literary vehicle and really his being a story of anarchy and patriarchal defiance—"

"SILENCE, POSEUR!" he said, and advanced on me. Before I could realize that I had not fully consented to it I was naked with a belt around my neck and being choked to the gods—he made me repeat "FUCK GOD, HAIL SATAN!" over and over again; he also was like, "YOU ARE JUST A FAGGOT HOLE FOR SATAN'S SONS!" to which I rolled my eyes. If this was Satan's best sex warrior it stood to reason why Satanism in general was such a PR nightmare. His stroke game was at about 58 percent and considering how much plot was involved I still felt that instead of fucking him I should have just, like, eaten a cheeseburger or goofed around on the internet. He had a box of condoms with inverted-pentagram insignia on them because apparently Satanists have their own brand of condoms? Condoms by nature seemed like such a lawful thing—why would a thrall to the Dark Lord even bother? But I said nothing and let him fuck me despite my mild latex allergy. He came in like three minutes and then showed me how to play Magic: The Gathering as promised, and though I never fucked him again I still to this day meet him every other Wednesday to play the game.

ED'S NAME
WRITTEN IN PENCIL

"YOU LIKE TO GET FUCKED, don't you?"

Mickey Johnson was seven and a half years old and sitting in the back of the school bus, beads of sweat collected all around his brow and temples. He wasn't even tall enough to see over the seat in front of him but he dared not look to his left 'cause there would be the bogeyman himself—Cortez Williams.

Cortez was eleven, foul breathed, and bigger than most of the kids at the elementary school (he had been held back three times). Mickey knew that if he looked Cortez in the eye he would be really starting trouble and the school bus was close to Cortez's stop. Mickey held his breath and closed his eyes, frozen. Cortez persisted.

"You be puttin' ding-a-lings in yo' mouth. You a faggot." Cortez reached over and started pinching Mickey's nipple to the point of pain over his Hulk Hogan T-shirt and then he bit him hard on the top of his ear.

The school bus was old and dilapidated—it was probably once the top of the line when it was made in the sixties, but some twenty years later, it was showing its wear. In the winter it was an icebox and now in the summer, one month shy of school being out, it was an oven. Even with all the windows rolled down. You could feel when the engine shifted in the floor of the bus, and at that moment, the engine gave a shift right as Mickey's heart did. As was the rule with this ritual, Cortez pressed his advantage harder and harder the closer he got to his stop.

"You be getting dicked in the butt." Cortez gripped Mickey by the privates so hard that Mickey started to cry. Cortez unlatched his hand and in a swift motion took Mickey's hand and placed it on the crotch of his shorts. Mickey noticed Cortez wasn't wearing any underwear—Cortez never wore underwear.

This is how it started.

Sometime at the beginning of the year, all the classes K–6 sat in the ball field for the beginning-of-the-year speech given by the principal. The rural elementary school boasted just under two hundred students so all the classes fit comfortably on around two acres of field. Earlier that summer a drunken transfer truck driver passed out at the wheel and smacked his rig right into the school, completely destroying the sixth-grade classroom. It was probably the most exciting thing that had ever happened in that town. Mickey remembered watching the evening news with his grandparents as a white woman with a perm and a Minnie Mouse T-shirt cried and held her crucifix necklace and pointed it at the camera, saying that it was a miracle that it happened during the summer while school was out and how "the Divine worked in mysterious ways."

Presently, the principal was talking some jazz about how he loved each and every student and how God protects. Mickey's mind was elsewhere. He wondered what it would be like to be sitting in a room quietly, then all of a sudden a truck ran through it—he couldn't picture it. He lost his train of thought and turned around. Sitting on his butt, legs folded in front, was Cortez in plain view, in little track shorts with no underwear. Mickey could see Cortez's penis. It gave him a nervous butterfly feeling and Mickey stared at it perhaps a beat longer than he should have. Cortez was sitting with his upper torso leaned back and propped up on his elbows: he wasn't really trying to cover himself, and he noticed that Mickey had noticed. The two made eye contact and Mickey quickly turned around.

Later there would be the first confrontation. Mickey's class and Cortez's class took bathroom breaks at the same time. A group of about fifteen boys would all wait in line. If the urinals were taken, the boys would crowd to the two doorless stalls that held a single toilet each. Three or four boys would urinate together at a time. To Mickey's left was Louis Gerbins, who everyone made fun of because he pulled his pants and underwear all the way down to his ankles to pee. Mickey undid his Superman belt and was relieving himself next to Louis when Cortez poked in the stall right next to Mickey, pulled down his track shorts (he seemed to favor track shorts), and let loose a stream of urine all across the belly of Mickey's shirt and the front of his jeans. When Mickey was asked what happened he blamed it all on Louis, who was promptly paddled, and Mickey was sent back to the bathroom to put on the change of clothes his mother insisted that he keep in his cubbyhole year-round.

It was now nearing the end of the school year and Cortez's attacks were becoming more frequent. Mickey always waited to see the town sign. "Welcome to Belle Mina," it said. It was a blip of a town off the I-65 highway. In the distant past the second governor of Alabama had made his residence there. Since the plantation slaves could not pronounce "Belle Manor," the town was named "Belle Mina" after that. Mickey didn't know this. All Mickey knew was that after the sign, the next stop was Cortez's house and that's when the torture would end.

It was a bus of thirty kids. Four white ones who were let off first, and then the Black students who were let off in the nooks and crannies of the farm town.

Cortez lived near the edge of the township in what they called "Camp Town"—several acres of cotton fields surrounded by woods. He lived on a plot of land that was all red clay (no grass grew there ever) and on the plot sat seven dilapidated trailers that all belonged to members of Cortez's immediate family. Cortez lived in one trailer with his grandmother and uncle, who was drunk all the time. The bus came to a stop.

"You gon' be my girlfriend," said Cortez to Mickey, and forced a kiss on his lips.

He looked at Cortez's hair. It was baby soft and blond on the tips, naturally. Cortez was a Black boy with blond hair. Now, someone had said Cortez's daddy was a white man. Nobody knew. But his mama had run away after he was born; she was last in New Orleans. It was understood that he was the son of one of the white men whose family owned the property Cortez's family lived on—that was the way Mickey's grandma had explained it. All Mickey knew was that Cortez intimidated him, and that his presence held Mickey in place like a magnet. Hate was not the first emotion Mickey could conjure when thinking about Cortez, though. Whatever "it" was, it rumbled in his stomach, like a fear or excitement, like those three seconds before a roller coaster hurled itself from a very high peak. Cortez unlocked his lips from Mickey's and Mickey exhaled hard. He was left alone with that feeling of relief that washed through him whenever Cortez exited the bus.

MICKEY LIVED WITH his grandparents and his dad. His parents were never married and his mother had moved up to Kentucky to finish her master's degree. "I'll come back when I can get a better job. I'll move us into a bigger house," she said, packing. The next day she kissed and hugged him within an inch of his life and left for school. Mickey's mother was studying speech pathology; it was explained to him that she was studying to help kids who couldn't speak well mute their *r*'s and clip their vowels, whatever that meant. He missed his mother, naturally, and the way she read to him each night. The last book he remembered her reading to him was *The Adventures of Huckleberry Finn*. It was his favorite. Sometimes Mickey had half a mind to grab his clothes and sail up a river—or at least he would, if he could swim.

When Mickey got home, the air inside his grandparents' house was smoke-filled, gamy, and peppery. His grandfather had come in drunk and was cooking a rabbit he had run over on the road somewhere; he was fond of running over animals with his car. He was making gravy for the meat and the thought of the poor rabbit in the pan was making Mickey sick to his stomach. "Is that dinner, Pa?" Mickey asked, really hoping it was not.

"No, this ain't for little boys, ya hear? This is for Dad. I'm taking you and your grandma to dinner in town tonight, so save your appetite."

Mickey saw through the window that his grandma was in the backyard taking clothes off the laundry line. If they were going out to eat later he knew that she would be taking her biggest purse to dinner, as always.

Mickey's granddad drove an older Cadillac—what year,

Mickey couldn't remember. It only played eight-track tapes and his granddad had to use a converter to play Mickey's favorite tape, a gas station compilation of sixties soul-pop tunes. Mickey sat in the front seat in between his grandparents and swayed his little body to "The Oogum Boogum Song," the Supremes, and "You've Really Got a Hold on Me." The tape had to be his favorite thing in the world.

The trio got up the highway on their way to Quincy's. Quincy's was a steak house and country-style buffet. Their signature was a type of yeast roll put on the table before your meal, and the commercial for the restaurant featured a cartoon anthropomorphic yeast roll with arms and feet singing, "I'm the BIG. FAT. YEAST ROLL." It was all certainly a carry.

Mickey's granddad had been a cook at Quincy's some years before and said he couldn't eat the food there because he knew it was all "utility-grade" meat—that is, animals they would find dead and turn into meat before rot set in. Mickey didn't care; he always ate from the ice-cream bar first anyway. He liked the way the pillowy melted marshmallow foam drizzled down his soft-serve vanilla ice cream, which he often topped with gummy bears. Mickey glanced over at his grandmother going to town on a full plate of fixings. He looked down in her purse and, as expected, she had already found a way to sneak a hellified amount of fried chicken in there, all wrapped up in napkins, the grease from the chicken turning the napkins translucent. His grandfather was smiling at them both, sipping iced tea.

The three rushed back home so his grandfather could catch *Jeopardy!* The living room was dark except for the bluish light of the TV. Mickey looked down at his Black skin. The luminous effect of the screen made it look simultaneously iridescent and even darker than it actually was. Right as he got lost looking at himself his father burst through the living room door.

Mickey's father was all about big entrances—you could feel the charisma of him six feet before he arrived. He said a quick hi to his parents, who didn't even look up from the screen to acknowledge their son. Mickey followed his dad to the bedroom they shared in the back of the house.

Mickey loved his dad. It was mostly his smell—a mix of alcohol, pork cracklings, and cheap cologne. He would sit in his dad's lap when he would play dominoes with the men at the pool hall in town, and lean his head against his dad's chest just so he could smell him. It was a very peaceful smell.

Mickey sat on the bed and watched his dad's nighttime preparty ritual (which happened most nights of the week). He would dash out of the shower, toss on cologne and deodorant and hair grease. After this he would always proceed to spray a grotesque amount of starch on his Levi's 501s and iron them till they were stiff as a board. His father sometimes called him "Mouse" ('cause his name was Mickey). "Yeah, Mouse, imma find you a pretty stepmama tonight! Look at the crease in these pants! You could fuckin' cut ya'self on 'em!" None of these stepmothers ever materialized, but either way, Mickey loved watching his father's nightly beauty rituals. He was less like a dad and more like an older brother. It worked.

His father threw on a pair of pristinely white Converse and a green Izod polo, grabbed the keys to his '76 Volkswagen Beetle, and hit the door. "See you when I get home, Mouse, stay up and wait for me, ok?"

"Ok, Papa," said Mickey. His father picked him up off the bed and hugged him tight and kissed him on the forehead. He sat him down and was off.

Mickey always wanted to tell his dad about Cortez but always kept the matter close to himself. For one, he didn't want his Father Bear thinking he was a punk, and two, he knew that any kid who snitched on another kid was a dead kid. If he got Cortez in trouble he would have to fight Cortez and all his scary-ass cousins for the rest of his life. It was all very lose-lose.

Mickey's grandparents had gone to sleep and he pulled out two VHS tapes from a pile by the TV. One was a bootleg copy of an hour of BET videos and the other was also a bootleg copy, of his favorite movie, *Flashdance*.

He put on the BET tape and rewound it to his favorite spot— the Janet Jackson "Pleasure Principle" video. What wasn't to love about Janet Jackson? She had it all: she had bangs, she drank water out of a bottle (this baffled Mickey), and she was a dancer who lived in a warehouse. Was this a thing? He cross-referenced it with Alex, the protagonist stripper / performance artist in *Flashdance*, who also more than likely drank water out of a bottle, but most definitely was a dancer who lived in a warehouse. All the evidence was clear; all the coolest people were dancers who lived in warehouses (he was on the fence about the bottled water part). As always, Mickey alternated the tapes and practiced the routines until 2:30 a.m., when his dad got home, and Mickey would curl up beside him and hear about all the gossip at the club.

The next morning Mickey missed the school bus. He and his dad were up talking too late. His father called in sick to work and took Mickey to breakfast and dropped him off at school ten minutes after the morning tardy bell had rung. He was late with a stomach full of Hardee's biscuits and strawberry jam. He felt satiated.

He stepped into Ms. Dickerson's class and spied the new boy—he and Mickey were wearing the same sleeveless gray ThunderCats T-shirt with a full print of Lion-O (the team leader) on the front and the red-and-black ThunderCats emblem on the back. In Mickey's head, immediate friendship seemed like the next step.

"My mom goes to Dollar General too!" exclaimed Ed, Mickey's new immediate best friend. He had this feeling in his stomach now, the same as when Cortez would bother him, only much more violent, yet sweet too, like three packets of Pop Rocks fizzing in his stomach all at once.

Ed was from Texas. Mexico before that. He was dark, but

not like Mickey. He was more medium brown, like a cinnamon color, as opposed to Mickey's indigo. He had an accent that Mickey had only ever heard on TV before.

He had a rattail and his bangs almost covered his eyes. Ed's father and mother both went to Athens State University, the college in the next town over; they were finishing agricultural degrees. Ed had no brothers or sisters. Both boys agreed that they wished they had "Cheetara" T-shirts (the female psychic feline warrior from ThunderCats). They also both agreed that they should share crayons all day.

After school Mickey sat sweating on the bus. Ed was right next to him. Ed's parents had moved into the renovated old post office in the center of town. This was along Mickey's route. Mickey had focused on Ed so entirely that he hadn't noticed that Cortez wasn't riding the bus that day.

The windows were all down on the bus and Mickey could waft Ed's smell—Dial soap and sweat. It had a sweet smell to it, different from his dad's, but still, a peaceful smell.

"I never talked to a Black person," said Ed, which he punctuated by putting his arm around Mickey's shoulder. Ed smiled big and removed his arm and they both sat close, elbow touching elbow, side by side. They both watched the cotton in full bloom as the bus raced through the fields.

The bus let Ed off and Mickey waved goodbye to him and then it hit. Cortez was nowhere to bother him.

He breathed a sigh of relief and sank back into his seat.

He almost wished Cortez could have been there to see his new friend Ed. He even fantasized about him and Ed beating Cortez up.

Mickey went straight to the room he shared with his dad. He wrote Ed's name on the wall in pencil and erased it over and over and over again.

The next day at school Ed didn't show up, and neither did Cortez. Both boys missed the next day and the one after that.

Ms. Dickerson explained to Mickey that Ed's parents had found more suitable housing near campus and he would start attending the elementary school in the town the next county over. He then heard from his grandmother that Cortez's uncle and cousin had been arrested and he was in New Orleans with his mom again. It was the end of the school year so none of it really mattered. There was a new feeling in Mickey's stomach now. It felt like the bottom was falling out of it.

Later that day on the school bus with neither predator to probe him nor friend by his side, Mickey let out a big sigh as the bus stopped to drop the other kids off. He was bored.

ACT II

100-PAGE
BREAKUP
LETTER

LETTER OF RESIGNATION

I AM FUCKING MY COWORKER'S HUSBAND.

I know that I am a horrible person. I don't know if I'm more horrible for doing it or for not giving a fuck that I am doing it—even the quandary of it all just overwhelms me.

I work at a nonprofit. I'm sitting at my desk in the back of the office, tucked into a corner. From this vantage point I can see all movement in the office, and so naturally I am masturbating at my desk.

I am watching the new receptionist, Arnold, who sits at the front of the office.

He just started college this year and works part-time. His

clothes are always tight, so tight in fact that I can often see the lining of his underwear through his pants. He is equal parts chubby and fit—he's built like a tenth-grade football player and his body is a constant source of inspiration for me. He looks like a human sausage packed tightly in respectable H&M off-the-rack wear, and all I can think about is getting inside his asshole.

Earlier this morning I saw him kiss his girlfriend goodbye and he had to stand on his tiptoes to meet her lips, as she is a good head taller than him. I could see that fat ass of his and his body in relevé. It sent me over the edge.

He's talking on the phone and I am jerking my dick to the sight of his tender-ass lips moving and I'm hoping that I can bust a nut before anyone else in the office turns around to see me. Three, two, one . . . mission accomplished. I don't even wipe the cum off my dick, I just quickly shove it back in my pants and fling all the cum on my hand onto the carpeted floor and rub it in with the bottom of my wing-tipped shoes. I roll my head back and take a deep sigh. There is something very liberating about masturbating in an office. But this feeling soon washes away and it's back to work, work, work.

I'm a data analyst at a nonprofit whose goal is to pair underage children in foster care with services. In and of itself, it sounds like a noble life but in truth I am surrounded by sketchy, burned-out, nonprofit employees. The office manager is this lady by the name of Sue Lauren—she had been a caseworker for years before moving into the lofty yet still underpaid position she holds now. I remember doing cocaine in her office with her at a Christmas party one year and she confided in me: "I was at my old job, hungover and helping this blind orphan cross the street and realized that I had always hated my job. Like, why did *I* have to be the person to help him?"

It's lunchtime, and I know this not by the clock but by the sight of my office buddy Sean, who's twirling gay as all fuck from the elevator and making a beeline to my desk. I am pretty sure that at some point I've seen this queen unironically skip through the office. As the saying goes, he's so gay Helen Keller could tell. I remember when he first started working at the center two years ago. Within half a day at the office I had him bent over the sink in the bathroom with my hand over his mouth so no one could hear the whimpering noises he was making while I was fucking him. This continued for a month or so until we were over it and now we are lunch partners.

Sean is thirty-nine, Pilipino, and therefore ageless—he doesn't look a day over sixteen and this is only punched up by his draconian skincare regimen and the fact that he's a middle-aged man and still dresses like a ho in his twenties. I can't tell what breezy and optimistic avenue of San Jose Sean grew up on and floated out of but it has to be a groovy one—this bitch is *always* feeling it. At lunch I can hardly ever get a word in edgewise during our "conversations," most of which are attacks of unsolicited advice from him. Advice on my clothing, career path, choice in neighborhood, and, sorely, my love life.

"I mean, we're both pushing forty, girl! I just want you to

find happiness like I did! You can't troll a bathhouse forever!" He is actually giggling as he says all of this and this is why I am fucking his husband.

We are walking back to the office and Sean is chatting me up and I am annoyed.

We have a small argument about the filmmaker Joel Schumacher and his claim that he had slept with ten to twenty thousand people. I made the argument that it was logistically improbable that that ever happened and Sean is dead set on convincing me it was completely plausible. "All you would have to do is sleep with two new guys once every two days for fifty years! *Simple!*" he chirps, staring me down, as if his assured eye contact alone should be the thing that convinces me.

I, being what one therapist jokingly referred to as a "clinical sex addict," am no stranger to the thought of wanting to be washed over by a nameless void of men, but the consistently unreliable variable that one can never count on in any sex scenario is other people. I know this from experience.

I became depressed in the period after my father died. When I flew back home to the East Coast to clean out his house, I happened upon a photo SD card of my dead father getting head, fucking random women, and jerking off. In my grief I jerked off to the content of the card for about a week and then, when that feeling no longer satisfied, I went to the bathhouse every day after work for a period of months. I would often get a room and leave the door open with a towel over my head, and would lie completely still and let anyone who wanted to fuck me. I can't say how many different men it was as I couldn't see them—what I do remember is one man inserting himself in me and a particular feeling of a water nozzle spraying in my butt. This man was urinating inside me and I took the towel off my head to see who on Earth this hooligan was. It was the man I would come to know later as Sean's husband. We exchanged numbers and continued to meet up until a point and then I didn't see him for a while.

I remember the first Christmas party that Sean brought him to and introduced him to me as his husband. We looked each other in the eye and said hi as if we had never met before, and by the end of the party the husband and I were wasted and sucking each other off in the alleyway behind the building. This was two years ago and we have continued on since.

WE ARE STILL WALKING and Sean is still mindlessly talking and I have a hollow feeling that he has never once noticed me not listening to him. But I forgive this transgression because it is comforting to have someone to walk with. I like walking with Sean because it is essentially like being alone or more accurately like being in company, though unnoticed.

I have always been in the practice of being unnoticed.

I am a middle-aged man, and slightly portly, my hair is prematurely graying and I wear boat shoes. No one takes the time to give me the once-over twice and I've possessed this gift since I was a child. My mother once explained to me that all through her pregnancy she would often rush to the doctors to check in on me because I would not move in her stomach for days. Upon arriving on the planet not much changed. My first memories of childhood are of spending much of my day stationary and talking to myself, and when I did move it was me playing hide-and-seek for hours with no one. I don't even recall an imaginary friend—it had always been just me.

But back to Sean.

Sean is, for all intents and purposes, an imaginary friend. Sometimes, just to test his listening, I say quite clearly (though in a hushed tone), "I am fucking your husband, Sean"—to which he always replies, "What did you say?" It's uncanny how much this man chooses to ignore me. I do the same to him often.

Sean and I are nearing the office and I unceremoniously break away—I'm sure he's so deep in thought that he won't notice that I am gone for another half block.

I take a sharp right and veer into the downtown mall and up to the eighth-floor bathroom, which is tucked into a corridor on the right of a department store.

I have had public sex in this bathroom ever since I have worked at this job. Sometimes I meet Sean's husband here and we fuck. Today I am waiting for anyone who shows signs of interest and I'm walking in and out long enough to not look like a fucking creep. I am looking under the bathroom stalls and seeing if anyone is tapping their foot suggestively. As I look, I am still stuck on the Joel Schumacher claim.

I too could take my best weekly average and multiply it by my sexually active years and get 780, but I know that number isn't right, and I guess it just illuminates how math is the most manipulated of all the sciences, and memory is even shakier. Plus, those numbers don't explain the time I've spent simply waiting for the event, or, sadly, the days when there was no one who wanted to fuck me at all.

Had Joel ever in his life had those days? The days when no one wanted to fuck him? If his number is correct then apparently not.

In my experience, there are the days where all you really do care about *is* the number. The number is the comforting thing, the thing you can actually take to bed. The act in and of itself, the fucking part, quite honestly there are days where it can't be over fast enough. Like, you just want to cum already to say you did it. Sex is just light points on a grid, stars in the Milky Way, but really, the ether holding them all together is the waiting. Just sitting around, waiting in some feces-scented bathroom hoping to get fucked.

I've now worked myself into a mood and I wait in the bathroom for basically anything until no one comes and so I'm another hour late for work but no one notices. No one comes to punish or rescue me.

THE NEXT DAY Arnold is not at work and I still manage to squeeze off two at my desk thinking about him before lunch. I think about him so much I feel like I owe him, like, a $400 gift card at the next office Christmas exchange.

After my second orgasm I sit at my desk and pretend to do

work until Sean comes up to whisk me away to lunch, where he is once again back on his bullshit.

In the span of fifteen minutes Sean manages to reference at least three times how much he likes to get fucked—I am looking at the ground and trying to wrap my head around who it is he is trying to convince. He is 5'6", demonically aerobicized, and wearing a (self?) bedazzled Abercrombie T-shirt ("It's vintage! I've had it since tenth grade!") and Puma loafers. Like, on what planet is his triflin' ass, chaotic bottom energy not visually centered enough? Must I always have to bear witness to his soliloquy of love for dick?

Somewhere all along the thought process of tearing my lunch buddy to shreds I begin to feel a secret shame come over myself. I feel like one of those "I don't mind what they do—as long as they don't talk about it" reverse-bigoted, whatever you would call it kind of people. I'm a little sick of myself. And besides, Sean is just playing his position. I look at his tight little body and sigh a bit—like, why *shouldn't* he be stuffed with dick all the time? I mean, what other purpose would he have in life? He barely graduated from college, he hates his nonprofit job, and our mutual futures look bleak as fuck—I understand why he dreams of fucking all day. I start staring a hole in him and my dick is hard again; I have half a mind to ask him if he wants to skip lunch and go fool around in a public bathroom but I know the answer will be yes so I am immediately bored by the prospect. But I do have this warm feeling inside knowing that

I work with a buddy who would readily entertain the idea, as it is always the small victories in life that speak power to truth.

We make it to lunch and Sean continues to talk about Joel Schumacher and his twenty thousand sex partners and I am silent. I think this rumor is for gay sluts what the story of Jesus must feel like for Christians—hearing it makes you feel all holy and gives you a feeling of purpose but if you sat down and thought about it you know that shit did not happen.

Or maybe I was just jealous?

I could easily think of countless people I wanted to murder, sure, but countless people in any given algorithm that I would go out of my way to fuck? Fuck no, no way. There isn't enough instant karma in the world that would make me that friendly. I was convinced that I simply didn't like people that much and there was no fucking way Joel Schumacher did, either. Joel Schumacher was a rich white man and by that definition alone I know he was very likely judgmental, cold, and self-segregating. I had worked for enough rich white men to know that they are not by design a *deeply* friendly bunch, and they are surely not friendly enough to casually fuck twenty thousand people. I decide that I have had enough of this lie and need Sean to shut the fuck up.

"Sean, I'm fucking your husband. I have been fucking your husband for some time now." I say it out loud as casually as one could imagine, considering that my stomach had sank into my asshole.

"I know you are, me and Mike are open—we talk about you all the time, we tell each other everything." Sean has not even looked up from his plate.

"You talk about me with him?! How do you talk about me?" I ask, even though I don't want to know.

"Oh, we talk about you with great care—he's fond of you, actually."

"I have to go, I'm going to be sick," I mumble, and as I exit the table I catch a quick glimpse of Sean's face that reads as a confused panic.

I am running back to the office and decide I want to leave this place and leave it for good.

I think about Sean's husband and how I barely even think of him as having a name, much less a title and duty, i.e., "Sean's husband." Like, ew.

I fucked this man a handful of times—after he pissed in me at the bathhouse we agreed on some dates and I went to his minimally furnished and overly neat apartment. We said nothing and somehow, I had felt suffocated by the vibe; I cannot tell you much more than that. But there was something too sobering about the coincidence of Sean and meeting this man all again. I wanted to pick apart all the projected reasons I would have around why basic bitches like Sean get wifed up and why jaded, judgmental borderline misanthropes like myself end up fucking in shit-scented public restrooms, but I didn't have to ask—I had already answered the question.

There had to be a hundred stray men in my Rolodex who

were whores like Sean's husband—that is, ever present yet faintly existing—but he was the one whose memory had come back to strangle me. It wasn't like I was in some indispensable place with lots of options—I was stuck at a nonprofit job, fucking my coworker and his husband. It was time to run.

I am packing my desk like a new fugitive ready to book it for his life, shutting off my computer and leaving a note that says SHE'S OVER IT on my desk. I am tossing all the self-help books I never read away like bad avocados. I am holding my book bag close to my body as if it contains valuable things, but it only hides a stapler and other supplies I stole from the office closet. No one in the office even looks up to notice me frantically escaping, and even in the perfect protective coverage of being ignored I still feel like my eyes are revealing too much of my inner worry, and in my mind, I sit at my desk, disheveled and breathing off beat. I opt for more psychic armor so I imagine I am sitting at my desk with a towel over my head.

MEANDERING (PART ONE)

HE WAS SURROUNDED BY BORING (yet STRONG) stray thoughts; they were clogging his ability to fix the mess. The mess of his room surrounded him.

"When did I *get* all this bullshit?"

It wasn't anything a bunch of clear plastic office-store boxes wouldn't fix, but it made him nervous nonetheless. He had been to the houses of responsible adults before and didn't really dig it; adulthood all seemed to be about boxes, mostly boxes, actually. He didn't want to compartmentalize anything else, and unlike all the people he knew, he felt he lacked that synapse in the brain that could easily label stuff. Most objects in his head were beyond classification, anyways. For example, a picture you didn't want to hide away but didn't want to be confronted with every day—where the fuck do you file something like that? Dear god, everything was like that and therefore deserved its own special place, and god forbid you ever own enough stuff, eventually there are special things covering every inch of everywhere and you become some well person trapped deep in the earth suffocating on sentimentality. A normal person would detest this room but the boy wasn't normal.

He preferred the choose-your-own-adventure stylings of a junk drawer or, even better, a junk room.

If you lived in a junk room, every so often you would look under something and find something else—an important memory you lost, and say, "AH!" or "Awwwww!" It was a lottery where you just kept fucking winning.

The summer before, he had worked as a mover and discovered the secret lives of the bachelors who lived in Tiburon. So many male bachelors in their fifties! Single men who lived in two-story duplexes packed to the gills with straight-up bullshit—this one man whose garage was all old answering machines and water skis that hadn't been fucked with since the eighties. The boy with the messy room wondered if this was the fate of all bachelors; does a lonely man just keep buying shit? Would we really all just go shopping? *Rad*, he thought.

He looked at his room and calmed down a bit; he had only one room's worth of shit, not two stories and a basement. It was all Fred Perry polos, Levi's, records, records, records. He lived with six roommates whose rooms looked the same. "I don't feel like an adult," he accidently said out loud.

But messy rooms were fine. He liked the two weeks it took to clean it up. He liked watching things go from chaos to order. It was godlike.

He was aware how the room had got into this mess. The month before had been the breakup. Supposedly it started over a missing Troggs record but really it was about the boy cheating on the other often. It turned violent and they took time apart. Three days ago, the attempted reconciliation turned violent again when his ex-boyfriend, Matthew, had come back over to talk it out. It didn't work.

At the end of the day he just figured he was no good for Matthew—the man wanted other things. He could look into Matthew's eyes and see that he wanted a white-walled, white-doored, white little house in the New England countryside. They would make their own jam together. Every time Matthew crawled on him at night he could see in his eyes how he wanted to make sweet boyfriend love. It made the boy sick. He went out at night and had nasty whore sex behind Matthew's back. Their circle was small—he knew who Matthew knew. He could say he was sorry but it was a lie. It was the only way he could get off. He still loved the previous man. It would never work.

The main problem with Matthew was that he had an English accent, so everything he said "sounded right," or at least reasonable. Unlike Matthew, everything the boy said sounded less than feasible and was punctuated with "like" and "you know what I mean?"

Again, it escalated and again one of his roommates came to intervene and again he was left alone in a dirty room.

That was three days ago. "A fight with my ex, and a walk to calm my nerves," he said, putting his bag in order.

He put a notebook in his tote bag and some pens. He was going to get wasted then get some writing done.

He trotted up the street fast, chest forward, and heavy-footed like a man who was trying very hard to walk away from a fight he had just lost. No one looked him in the eye.

Now up on the corner was the old bar, the place he used to go—he'd even DJed a party there. Like every goddamn thing else on the old block someone had bought it, painted it an offensively inoffensive earth toned color, put salvaged wood and air plants every fucking where (the "newest" modern), and charged ten extra dollars for drinks.

All the drinks had names now.

He wandered in. What was once a whiskey and soda at this bar was now called a "Peter Paul" and made with in-house barrel-aged whiskey and in-house fermented aromatic bitters. The poor boy could only stomach so much "newness." A drink that had once cost five dollars and took fifteen seconds to make now cost eleven dollars and took two minutes. Just how far were they going to take this bullshit? He was afraid to ask.

He remembered the days it had been a "punk" dive bar

(i.e., a shittier and cooler version of itself). He remembered when all the booths had holes in them and there was graffiti everywhere, some of it even dating back to the late eighties. It looked dirty, it felt dirty—it *was* dirty. His mind switched quickly to how ok the "newness"—and the gentrification in general—felt, but then on the flip side was the flawed reasoning of loving something or thinking it "authentic" just because it seemed to be surviving neglect and abuse. He wondered if this was how he saw *himself*. Then the scene in his head switched back to the fight with his ex-boyfriend.

He noticed that he and Matthew acted the way one would expect two weathered queens dating in adulthood to act. He couldn't characterize all the dysfunction exactly, but he could calculate that it was a mix of compulsion, exclusion, obsessiveness, jealousy, infidelity, always wanting to "outsmart" each other, and, amid all of this, an extreme sense of separation anxiety when the other was away.

He turned to a page in his journal he had written about Matthew while he was asleep next to him—Matthew had somehow passed out and the boy was still high on drugs.

March 22, 20__

My heart is beating out of my chest and Matthew is
sleeping. I want to wake him, confront him, and accuse
him of taking the last Xanax but I know that it will lead
to trouble. I see him heaving his chest rhythmically
like an angel—I fucking haaaaaaaate him. I hate how

comfortable he is in the world. He derails all my concrete thoughts with platitudes, like "everything happens for a reason" or "that's just how the cookie crumbles," and, my least favorite, "you're just high on drugs and paranoid." I don't know how to explain to him that I'm not *just* high on drugs. I AM DRUGS . . .

He was maybe beginning to see Matthew's side.

No sooner had his thoughts stopped on drugs than who should walk into the gentrified bar other than Martha, everyone's favorite dyke drug dealer. He hated that bitch. She represented newness in the same form that overtook the once cool, now spruced-up bar. He remembered when drug dealers in the city were plentiful and you could just drop by their house, collect, and get the fuck on with your life. Martha was a particular breed of drug dealer, one that insisted that in order to sell to you, the two of you MUST be friends and sit and gab. Normally it grossed him out but he needed to unload about his failed relationship, and who better to talk to about a failed relationship than a dyke high on coke? The two of them sat there until the bar closed and the boy scored a bag as he was leaving, on his way to the apartment of one of the boys he cheated on Matthew with, or maybe he would just walk around aimlessly, like a story or love affair that had a strong start and stake at the beginning but toward the end just meandered.

THE BOYFRIENDS (INTERPRETATIONS)

Boyfriend #7 / Nicholas

Let's say for a moment you find yourself confined in a room of fractured rays of light (or we could say "little rainbows" to make them sound prettier). Now, would you feel empowered? Or like you were being attacked? I found no way to answer when a friend confronted me with this autobiographical question and revealed that the protagonist in the story for sure had felt attacked. She also asked me to bear with the protagonist, as he was not always easy to love. As my friend explained it: "Well, it's very easy, easy, easy to love the easy to love . . . isn't it?"

Boyfriend #33⅓ / Oscar

I drink firewater, often and late at night. Double-barrel—like a shotgun—and knock down every evening like a building past its prime making way for the new. Usually after midnight (after the fourth, fifth, sixth shot)—that's when he comes to me. (I come back to me.) Fresh from a blackout dream, like a ghost I'm not afraid of anymore. I see him in the mirror and I recognize him. The boyfriend beyond? The boyfriend within? No—he's real. You could just eat him up. There's a feeling of fleetingness with him. I've tried to escape before. To the canals in Amsterdam, artist in exile–style. But it feels like a fabrication on my part. (My exile was self-imposed. No one begged me to do it.) Why does it feel like this has to happen? I wish I could explain better . . . He felt the days creep like an old muscle car, gunning its way up the highway. He was in the back seat between two lovers. Ain't love grand? In the nighttime, one of the lovers shakes violently—it happens all the fucking time. He wakes up in a panic of red all over his brown face. He looks at me calmly and says, "I had a dream they were coming for me again and I couldn't escape with my true love." That statement cuts deep. True. Love. He says. Just by themselves the words "true" and "love" are pretty sturdy concepts. Put together they can knock down any man who's lonely enough to believe a lie as long as it's said *politely*. But back to the lover. This fake dream lover he was dreaming of. This fig of his imagination. Am I really fucking jealous of this ghost man? I am. "TRUE LOVE"?! DAMN! WHAT ABOUT ME, BITCH?! I feel as useless as a paperweight now, in stark contrast to the weightless feeling I get when I sleep next to him. These people who are coming for him in the dream—he fights them. But if the dream were *mine*, I would probably let them take me. It seems more reasonable than waking up all the time, and then maybe one could finally know thy enemy. I guess?

Boyfriend #0.000001 / Theo

It had been easy to ❤ him. What was not to ❤? I would see his Black blank flesh caressed in my nigger sheets of dawn; he would be always burrowing below the sheets. Relaxing his way into fetal position, the blanket wrapped all over his head and feet. It seemed that it became easier and easier for him to forget the things he had promised me. Like the rock I was, I parted the bedsheets in a pillowy white truce of surrender, his body slamming into my root chakra like a thunder god of undetermined ethnic origin. For the moment I pretend to be transformed by prompts and lies like any out-of-work actor whose ego demanded a paycheck. Let's say for instance, if by magic, and very suddenly, some small part of the eternities we are wrapped in could agitate the dark particles and turn time into a loop (or rather, picture a loop here—it's hard to get the right picture sometimes). As sure as our love had found its way into the dark one night, it evaporated as soon as the light switch clicked on.

Boyfriend #71 / Sagar

I felt raw. He had left me gagging for it . . . the truth. This had been the same mistake I always made, that is, expecting more: this was the last time I would bother myself with trying. I was annoyed by being imprisoned every time he touched me. Would this touch be different? The one that would be here for the day but gone for the week? I tried to tell him, but there was never much breathing room in the cadence of his fucking voice; no matter what—I was always drowning in him. Would it forever mean nothing at all? I wanted to be something else when he looked at me. A walking fiction. I wanted fake teeth, a fake accent, a fake sense of knowing where it was leading. I understood soon I was a liar, i.e., an actor.

Boyfriend #4/4 / The Drummer

What does love feel like? I'd imagine a rush, or, as a poet once put it, "twenty million tom-toms"—either way? I went to an artist lecture with my boyfriend the drummer and I remember the artist saying specifically, "Incoherence: the point where you are in the middle of making something and it no longer looks like art to you"; my butthole puckered when she said it and I looked to my boyfriend for eye contact, because what else is a boyfriend for but to share in mutual epiphany? That nigga was sleep as fuck. I even tried to decipher incoherence in his snoring, but no, he was all rhythm, even in his dreams. His snoring read like little kitten purrs of breath. It even read like drum tablature: left, right, left, right, right-right-left triplet, etc. We walked home in the streetlights and I saw the pattern in his steps—left, right, left, right, right, right, left. He wore all black like his teacher, a jazz master from some forgotten decade whose records he always played when I was walking naked around his apartment. His beard was thick like a Black man's and without it he looked Arab—"My mother is Black," he explained. The white man whose record was always playing when I was naked is his father. If incoherence truly is the point where art no longer looks like art to you then I guess a drummer can never be a real artist because even an incoherent beat is still a beat—no drum strike is ever truly out of place—even when it tries not to be. "You never stop looking like art to me," I said, all curled up, naked and lighting a joint under his black-clad body, and he held me for three more beats that hold space into forever.

THIS DAY AND
MANY MORE

I WAS JERKING OFF to the sound of my English roommate getting fucked. His trade always comes in the morning and I can always spy them through the blinds of my window, jogging up our front steps.

This trick in particular is an older Black man, looking to be in his late fifties. He is wearing brown polyester pants, a printed-satin fake–Louis Vuitton long-sleeve button-up, white snakeskin cowboy boots, and a matching white snakeskin cowboy hat. His hair is a shock of white afro smashed under his big-ass crown of a hat. He looks tall, like 6'2", has a gut but is otherwise muscular. He's hot and looks like he could make a bottom's dreams come true—you can tell his old ass has had a lot of practice.

My roommate intrigues me. He is a conventionally attractive boy, he could, as the pecking order goes, be a lot more selective than he is—the diversity of his trade is virtually unchartable. But no, he's a ho, like a *real* ho, like he will fuck virtually any man in the neighborhood who asks nicely; I have an undying respect for him because of that. If it weren't for the fact that 30 percent of his trade look like for-real serial killers I might even be jealous of him.

I hear him getting fucked hard, bed squeaking and shit, and he's making these elevated, open-vowel sounds; he is having a good time.

I, however, am furiously stroking my dick until I remember that I can't remember the last time I had fun having sex—this boner-killing thought, of course, kills my boner.

I have not left the bed in three days. There is a handle of whiskey by my bed. I am not celebrating.

The bed is beginning to smell but I am not bothered, I just open the window and turn on the ceiling fan. I love my bed because no one can hurt me here.

The open window reminds me of that saying, "Where God closes a door, He opens a window," but all I can think about is, like, *But wait, the window is on the fifth floor and the house is on fire*. To which the Almighty replies, "That's just some GOD humor—good luck!"

I can hear my neighbor who hates me dig through our

garbage; my landlord hired him to "look after the block." He sweeps and collects the trash of everyone for virtually pennies on the dollar and has taken to referring to me as "that uppity Black *faggot*" to all the neighbors. When informed of this I simultaneously was ready to kill and also chuckled to myself; "uppity Black faggot"—like, where was the lie?

I came home early one morning on a shit ton of blow and hammering a grip of vodka—I saw him rifling through the garbage cans and I confronted him: "YOU. CALLED. ME. A. FAGGOT," I screamed as I crouched to the pavement in tears, dropping and breaking my almost-full liter of vodka. He was so fucking uncomfortable that he apologized. His apology, as forced as it was, still felt good, but every time he comes in the yard I have this burning desire to put on a rainbow-flag cape, scarf, and matching socks (only) and jerk off furiously at him. I know this is a pipe dream—if I couldn't even bust a nut to the sounds of my roommate getting fucked, how was I supposed to get it up for that?

Half of the handle of whiskey is gone and it's only 10:00 a.m. I try to piece together where the time went.

At 8:00 a.m. my roommate's trick showed up; he left by 9:00. At 9:30 my asshole neighbor came and left, and fifteen minutes ago my roommate also left. I am finally all alone.

I woke up at 7:00 a.m. from this nightmare I have where I'm riding in a car and take off my seat belt to pee in a bottle. The brakes slam, and I fly in slow motion through a windshield. One would hope that after crashing through a windshield in a nightmare that something poetic would happen, like you turn into a dove, or like that dove turns into Oprah and, like, takes you for ice cream or In-N-Out. This nightmare lacked poetry because all I remembered was waking up alarmed in a pool of wet, cold sweat.

It felt like I was refusing my life; I was exhausted from the task of having to respond to stimuli. I had fucks left to give, of course, just not this week, and perhaps even the next. It was going to be a slow burn for sure.

I had left the bed earlier that week and it ended in a fight.

I went to the movies with my friend Mitch. We watched some French flick where two teenage boys beat the hell out of each other until the point where they mutually realize that they are "secretly" homosexual and in love.

In this one scene, they lose their virginity to each other. The scene flashes to the next day and the two boys are cuddled up together in bed, their naked bodies kissed in sunbeams on pristine white sheets.

Both boys were specimens—puberty is being very kind to them. They mutually boasted lean builds, no acne, and, judging from the clean white sheets still covering the bed, even their fucking colons were perfect too.

The first time I got fucked I remembered the white sheets under me looking like a fucking murder scene, like someone had just slaughtered a cow.

I made the mistake of telling my friend Mitch that I felt like whoever made that movie had done it just to fuck with me (yes, me *specifically*).

Mitch, being the ever-understanding type, said that I was being (as he kindly put) a "fat, jaded WHORE!" and yes, I should be happy for these two fictional French supermodels who somehow (in rural France, no less) found a way to beat the odds and find each other. Was the entire fucking world trolling me?

The last time I got laid, an older gentleman followed me home for seven blocks one night. I refused his advances outside the bar where he was waiting in his parked car. I stumbled home drunk and realized he had been following me. I went to confront him. As I walked to the car he removed his huge-ass old man dick from his pants and started jerking it at me and I immediately remembered how lonely I was. I let him fuck me in his car in an alleyway. He then requested that I dress in drag the next time we meet. I explained this all to Mitch. "This is the reason that movie makes me upset," I said.

Mitch told me to try meditation, and the mere mention of the word "meditate" sent me into a blind rage. I accused him of having rich parents and have not spoken to him since.

My response to stimuli is getting slower and slower, and for good measure I pop half a bar of Xanax—it's hardly noon and already this day is overwhelming.

I sit in bed waiting for the drop to hit me, that split second where you look up and realize that you are very, very sleepy.

I sit, feeling chemically peaceful, and all the thoughts in my head are like cursive letters written in fountain-pen ink on fancy paper. The harder the drop hits the more the cursive letters begin to slur and melt off the page, ink running like someone had spilled water over it. I am out like a light.

I WAKE UP to a vicious racket and someone is pushing and pulling me frantically in my sleep. I come to groggy as all hell and my vision is slightly blurred—I can hardly make out the time on my bedside clock: 2:13 a.m. I have been asleep for fourteen hours.

I click my lamp on and it's my other roommate, Steven. I hate Steven because he is a flaming piece of human garbage. He has lived off unemployment for the past year and somehow manages to drink even more than I do. I'm sure at this point his mental state is even more corroded than mine. He has spent the last three and a half years threatening to kill himself over the unrequited love of some boy whose name I don't remember. There was a time when the unrequited-love boy lived in the house for a while and every night they would get into some form of fight and Steven would chase after the boy crying and yelling, running out into the street in his underwear and crouching on the outside sidewalk in tears until the English roommate or I would go collect him. He is a horrible white person and I wish death upon him—and it seems I might get my wish.

I look down and notice that both of his wrists are slashed

and dripping blood onto my vintage Hello Kitty rug. I am immediately caffeinated with hate and vengeance. I don't think he understands that that rug means more to me than his life. I have half a mind to go back to sleep and let his punk ass die but of course I'm all like, "OH MY GOD!!!!! BABY, ARE YOU OK?!"

"I TRIED TO KILL MYSELF—CALL MY BOYFRIEND!!!" he says, half sobbing, half screaming.

Even with this many stimuli I still manage a slow-motion eye roll at this bitch. Like, call your "boyfriend"? Really, bitch? Not, like, the hospital? Having been in bed all day and slightly amused by the fact that there is a person who has even more problems than I do, I get up to really inspect the situation. The slashes on his wrists are not deep—he just needs some attention. I make him some tea and wrap up his bandages and muster, in my best mammy voice: "Now, honey, are you sure you want me to call whatever the fuck his name is? He's only going to call the police on you and you're going to spend the rest of the next day in the psych ward," I say in a whisper, pouring the hot tea.

"CALL. ERIC. NOW. GODDAMMIT!!!!" he screams, and throws the pot of tea across the room.

I go and dial the boy, who in turn dials the cops, who in turn come and arrest my roommate after he gets violent with them. I go back to sleep and wake up with a series of messages from Steven decrying that "Eric had me arrested" and "we have to call the local news station and tell them I'm being unfairly held."

I sigh and hold my breath just long enough to notice the sun is up, and I hear the rustling of the trash outside. The neighbor is back, digging through our recycling, and I fight the urge to flash my dick at him. Instead, I pour myself a modest drink and turn on cartoons. This too shall pass, though I am not leaving the bed again today, and perhaps not tomorrow.

HOOKER BOYS
(PART TWO)

I WAS VISITING MY GRANDMOTHER in Alabama one summer and marveled at how much the digital age had propelled the likelihood of getting dick in the dusty backwoods towns that populated this quadrant of the state. The entire county had become a virtual whorehouse overnight.

This one cat hit me up while I was taking a nap at my grandmother's house after church.

"Do you want an 80 or 90 massage?" said the message.

"Fuck yeah I do!" I responded.

He lived fifteen minutes up the highway, and when I got to his house I was taken aback by the scene.

It was a dirty apartment with clothes everywhere. The man did not look like his pictures. In fact, he looked like death. He had a frozen expression and a frozen vibe in general; like, it took him a noticeable amount of time to think and form sentences. He had track marks from shooting up all over his arms and legs, and his left leg was swollen and infected. He was limping on it.

About that time two preadolescent boys came storming into the apartment. They both referred to him as "Dad."

"We have to wait till my boys go to boxing practice, then we can fuck," he explained.

Heaven help me, I stayed because I am nothing if not the worst mix of willfully nonjudgmental and horny.

The boys left on a Boys and Girls Club bus that honked for them outside.

The man waved his sons goodbye, closed the front door, and pulled out his dick, which seemed to be the only thing about him in working order. He got me on all fours and let loose something wild, but I was startled by the way he kept repeating "I'll eat your ass for an extra twenty dollars." I wanted to unpack that statement but I was too busy getting fucked in the ass real good, arching my back and licking my lips and all things of that nature; then I came.

I put my clothes on and tried to leave when he blocked the door.

"Where is my ninety dollars?!" he said, looking frantic.

"Come again?" I said, in this what-the-fuck-did-you-just-say-to-me kind of tone.

"I said in my message do you want an eighty or ninety massage. I just massaged your asshole right now—where's my money?" He pushed me back and stood in front of the exit to the apartment, suddenly menacing.

I explained to him that I assumed he meant minutes and not dollars and that real hookers say things like "looking for generous" in their ad or at the very least post a dollar sign. I almost had the nerve to say that if I *were* to pay for sex, he (though a lovely person) wouldn't be my first pick, but decided not to talk shit to a junkie who might actually kill me.

We somehow agreed on twenty dollars (as it was all I had in my bank account). He grabbed me by the arm and escorted me to the ATM located at the end of his street.

I could only imagine that his street was "the ho stroll"; cars kept stopping and eyeballing us closely, and with his hand around my arm like this it must've looked like I was under pimp arrest. It was emasculating.

We got to the gas station and I had half a mind to scream like a white woman that he was holding me hostage, but it felt like that could be a massive misfire. Also, all I could think about were those two sweet little boys and their dismal fucking circumstances and hoped that maybe five dollars of the money would go to them.

I gave him the money and left the gas station a free man,

save the rude-ass comment he hurled at me from the opposite side of the parking lot, walking away with junkie bloodshot eyes and furiously limping.

"NEXT TIME DON'T PLAY WITH A NIGGA, NIGGA," he screamed.

BOYFRIEND #19 / THE WHITE BOY WITH DREADLOCKS

THERE ARE PERIODS OF MY LIFE that roll through me hazily. Not like an apparition, more like that moment a cartoon villain gets hit in the head with, say, an anvil or whatever, and all he sees is stars—my life was all flashbacks that never materialized.

I woke up to a spider crawling on the floor and I was reminded of this white boy I dated a while ago with these long-ass dreadlocks. I remembered that every time he was on top of me his dreads would graze my face and it felt like a nest of spiders crawling over me. I was too young to understand how this feeling would stain me permanently.

We met at a liberal arts college in the Midwest. It was freshman year and we mutually didn't know we were gay until we were drunk and had each other's dicks in our mouths at the student union hall one night at 2:00 a.m.

By junior year his dreads were in full bloom and I didn't think to tell him he should cut them (because I am nothing if not willfully nonjudgmental) or that I was certain that Jah hated him (it was the nineties and these convos weren't nearly as prevalent).

Either way later that year I dropped out of school to follow him whilst he was following Phish and Burning Spear (respectively) on tour. We ate up his trust fund on organic orange juice, gas for the Jeep, and acid. During that period, I had fucked under a blanket of stars in the Grand Canyon some nine or ten times, swam in secret watering holes in the Appalachians, and saw longer stretches of highway between California and North Carolina than I ever knew existed. It would not last.

A year and half later I was sitting around a fire in a drum circle in Colorado. I was washed out on acid and very drunk—at the apex of my trip I felt the hand of the ancestors tap me on the shoulder and say, "Girl, take your Black ass back to college—you don't even like these people. He just fucks good."

I snapped to my senses and woke up the next morning and showered (for the first time in like six months), cut my hair, and took a Greyhound back to our school to reenroll. At the bus station I tried to convince the dreadlocked white dude to come back to school with me and that we should probably switch our majors to like business or computer science.

I saw the look of judgment in his eyes and I knew immediately that he was going to say some busted shit, and I was right.

"I can't follow you back to Babylon," he explained, like completely fucking serious. "It's like Jerry said, man—short time to be here, and a long time to be gone." He broke down crying and hugged me. I went back to school and we stayed in touch for a while and by 2002 he finally cut those fucking things. I think he's a librarian now or something. He even apologized for the whole dreadlock Phish period eventually and every once in a while, I look him up and torture him with a joke.

Q: Where do hipples fuck and how is it?

A: IN TENTS MAN, INTENSE!

EARLY RETIREMENT

HE HAD ADOPTED THIS INSANE new beauty practice of rubbing Preparation H on the bags under his eyes. He was trying to scrub that puffy, confused, alcoholic look right off his face—it burned to all hell but goddamn if it didn't work. There had to be some kind of fancy, faggy, antiaging, anti-inflammatory something or other at a boutique in San Francisco that, like, smelled nice and blended into the skin in a less severe way. But these days he could barely make it to the corner store, much less downtown San Francisco.

The trolley cars bothered him, the European tourists giving him that what-are-*you*-doing-here look on the street both-

ered him, effort in general bothered him—put all th
together and what was left was a tube of hemorrhoid cī
purchased at the Grocery Outlet for $1.50. He still smelled
like alcohol in the morning but at least his face didn't look all
fucked-up. It was a small victory that would have to do.

He threw on shades and thought, *Why am I doing this?*
Then, *Wait,* how *am I doing this?*

The last couple of months he had started sleeping with
his feet hanging out of his second-story window. It helped to
correct his shiftless moving around in bed, and as a result he
could hear the cars out by the highway in the night. He started
to have dreams that he was peacefully underwater—but he
knew it was his brain reinterpreting the cars roaring past.
From a distance, the hum of the highway sounded like waves
crashing into land. From his bed, he would pull the covers over
his head and dream of being in the ocean. Alone and at peace.

It had been a hard stretch.

He was an actor and had got a job that summer as the lead
of this god-awful play, some drama about a murderer in a min-
ing town during the gold rush. It bored him to tears and he hit
the bottle real hard one night before the show, ended up black-
ing out onstage and being removed from the play the next day.
It was not the first time this happened.

He relayed the story to his friend Mark over the phone.

"I got drunk and embarrassed myself in front of a bunch of
prominent white neoliberals," he offered.

"Again?!" asked Mark.

"Again," he explained. "The stage manager was this hippie who told me I would never work in this town again! I broke down and cried." Real tears welled up—he could feel them leaking through the film of the Preparation H.

Mark kept his cool. "I mean, that's nice of her to threaten you and all but keep in mind you never really worked there before—who gives a flying fuck?! Meet me and the boys for lunch," he demanded.

He and Mark were brothers of sorts. Some decade and a half ago the two of them were cast in a TV show on a fledgling gay channel about the lives of four single Black gay men in L.A. It was a big to-do—audiences loved it, and he basically played the Black version of all the white queens he hated. He had been working on some horrible avant-garde play in San Francisco at the time when his agent called him with an offer for the part of "Jonathan"—muscular, thirty-three, nonurban Black, hippie wallflower type. It seemed easy enough. He had been having problems getting acting gigs not reading as "urban"—every role called for a strong masculine Black man with confidence and all the answers, and he couldn't fake that even for a paycheck. The role of Jonathan felt tailor-made—after all, he grew up in Encino.

The show was so uniquely Black (or as "Black" as white West Hollywood tastes would allow) that no one noticed the characters for what they were: really shitty muscle queens from L.A.

He hoped at first they would mirror the Spice Girls and

each have some form of distinct personhood (he wanted to be the dark-skinned "woke" one), but there was no such luck. Instead they were four leads who all mirrored one another like quadruplets; the running catchphrase of the show (said by all of them in unison) was "Ew! He's fat!" (Cue laugh track.)

He made semidecent money for the price of his soul and did what all reasonable G-list "celebrities" on G-list sitcoms did: he stumbled into cocaine and alcohol addiction. The show was over before the third season and he stayed on drinking. He moved back to San Francisco broken as all hell and chased jobs in regional theater while, during harvest season, he worked in the pot farms up north.

Mark himself had moved to San Francisco recently—he was working as an agent now, developing talent.

I hate the idea of meeting these faggots for lunch, he thought, getting ready. The problem was, he despised Mark's habit of always dragging boys he was fucking to brunch for an awkward meet and greet. And considering his foul mood it all felt a bit extra today.

Still, he threw on shades—it was time to meet these faggots for lunch.

Upon arriving he quickly ordered an "Irish Health"— Jameson whiskey and green tea on ice with simple sugar (a splash of Baileys if you must).

"Ah . . . ," he said, ". . . now I feel better." He slammed it and then ordered a double of the same.

Mark brought two queens he'd had sex with the night before. One boy was a blond and the other had a birthmark on his face.

Mark was dominating the conversation, as always. He had a way of taking a conversation and boiling it down to its essentials—his stories always led back to sex and/or violence. It never failed. This particular brunch he was explaining how he had recently been robbed south of Market Street.

"I had on a thousand-dollar watch, had all my credit cards on me, seven hundred dollars in cash I owed my roommate, and an extra-large cheese pizza I ordered from the place on the corner. So, I see this big Black muscle queen walking towards me from Twelfth Street. Big ole uncut dick swinging to the gods in his track pants and I'm staring him down like, 'Wanna fuck?' He rolls up on me and the last thing I remember is him punching me in the head. Anyway, I wake up about thirty minutes later, and I know it's thirty minutes later 'cause I still had my watch on, my credit cards, *and* the cash—the only thing missing was THE PIZZA!!"

The boy with the birthmark spit up his Jack and soda. The blond boy asked me what I did.

"I was an actor but I failed. Now I work in agriculture, seasonally," I said, not looking him in the eye. "I'm in between trips."

"You mean you grow weed?" he pressed.

"Yes."

They all got drunker and went to Mark's. The men got naked on the bed, but he felt apart, too drunk and sad to achieve an erection. There came a point where the merry trio was all having sex on top of him and he rolled over and pulled the covers over his head. He wanted to be underwater again.

HE HAD TO KILL ALL THE BOYS. This was his job. A boy plant's pollen can travel up to half a mile away and, with one drop of it, the whole crop would get seeded. Pot with seeds is unsalable and the farm would lose money.

Other times, even without the boys, there were girl plants that could change sex—they would drop balls and start getting all the other girls pregnant. This was corrected by killing and disposing of all the new boys right as they "dropped balls" (seed sacs).

He had been on the mountain for a while now. The exact number of days he could not tell—time blurred so much up there. His task was repetitive, but he loved being alone. Just him, the plants, the drying room (the only built structure on the property), the hum of the gas generators, and his two guns.

There was a period when he would go to random farms and trim for strangers but it didn't last long. It was a particular form of hell being stuck three hours from nowhere in the California backwoods with white hippies; they all smelled bad and had Ganesh tattoos. They insisted that he "think positively." He hated that shit. He had scored the right gig eventually, with this private small farm that he worked alone until the fall trimmers came to finish manicuring the whole crop.

There was a fussy creek cutting through the hills that he bathed in in the mornings—the icy coldness of it stung his balls. No soap could be used in it, as it would pollute the river. All his other supplies and actual drinking water were kept in a slender kitchen with a separate entrance on the back side of the drying room. He had to shit in a hole in the ground.

The goal was to get all the weed cut and dried before the rainy season started in early winter. Two years before, the rain had started early and had molded all the plants, which didn't begin to cover how damn miserable he had been in the tent. He made a pallet to sleep on in the drying room this time around.

He stayed in the room even after the rain was over.

At nights, alone in the drying shed, the landscape outside had the dark glow of moonlight. The moon had put a soul filter on everything. The hum of the gas-powered generator reminded him of the underwater sound of the highway cars he could hear from his bed in the city. He was alone in the expansiveness. He felt like a nature god.

IF HE REALLY HAD TO THINK ABOUT IT, he had never wanted to be an actor. Not really, that is; in his memory, it had all happened upon him. On a whim, he had stormed the stage when he was five—it was a one-man coup.

His older cousin was eight or nine and participating in her elementary school beauty pageant—he was sitting in his Sunday church suit in the audience of the elementary school gymnasium next to his auntie. He noticed all the girls in pretty dresses, lit up onstage, and the applause every time the girls twirled about.

When one contestant departed the stage, he saw it empty and knew he should be there. He snuck from under his auntie and ran up the side steps and placed his little body midstage. He couldn't see the faces of the audience (perhaps an early indicator of his nearsightedness). Then came the roar of applause. He knew he had done something right because everyone was clapping for him. Right as the shock wore off, his little face produced a smile—just in time for his auntie to come rip him off the stage by his right hand.

"BOY, YOU KNOW YOU KNOW BETTA!!!!" she exclaimed in a yelled whisper in his ear as she led him down the stage stairs. He couldn't even hear her. The smile on his face lasted for days.

All he wanted, he realized, were the stage lights and the applause; the acting itself was just the driver holding the carrot in front of the donkey. He figured that if culture had allowed for a butcher, a baker, or a candlestick maker to get stage lights and applause, he would have easily been that, too. But life, being what it was, made him an actor.

His mother had always hated his profession; she thought it was too common. She barely even congratulated him when he got on a network show. She wanted him to be a teacher and she eventually got her wish.

There was a time he spent teaching acting workshops at regional theaters after the TV show got canceled—there were a great many people who couldn't act. He marveled at how all reluctant thespians had the same complaint: "I don't like being watched." He knew this statement was a cop-out. He could usually cure the novice actor with one sentence. "You're not afraid of being watched—you're afraid of *watching* yourself be watched." The student would always get this confused look and then more often than not a series of breakthroughs would start.

In his eyes, the spewing of words was the easy part; it was the blocking that killed or illuminated the expression, the business of what to do with the hands or feet when trying to convince others that you are someone else, movement always being the pure indicator of how truthful one was being.

He had never been a good actor, just a very committed one. He was like Robert Downey, Jr., or Mel Gibson—he had committed in acting to being himself. Acting had given him the license to be himself. The context, accent, or historical backdrop could change play to play, but he stayed wrapped up in his typecast: a fragile yet strong (or fake brave) and always spiraling man.

In acting he hid behind his characters to put distance between him and the audience. It was like the first night he stepped onstage when he was five. As far as he was concerned, there was only the holy trinity of him, the stage lights, and the void. It was perfect freedom. It would not be forever.

He began to notice it. It was small at first, but then it grew.

It was something he had warned others against but slowly was unable to reconcile in himself; he started to notice himself being watched. It was the beginning of the end, and the death was sudden. Out of fucking nowhere one day, the audience all had faces, eyes, and expectations. Without warning, something internal had changed. After the show got canceled, he retreated to the tepid world of Northern California live theater; all bit parts with no infrastructure for advancing. His artistic fatigue culminated the night he blacked out onstage the final time. Even his meltdown was mundane.

First it started with two celebratory shots before each stage performance, then four, then half the bottle. Before long he had been fired for the first time from a stage production for reeking of alcohol onstage.

He had quit for a bit and even went to AA—it seemed like a start but he descended again. The time after was harder. The second and third time you fail is always worse; there's the voice that asks, "Am I really choosing to be this person?" The realization felt like death, or like being underwater, but not in a peaceful way.

Up north, after his meltdown, he sat at the general store in town looking at a bottle of whiskey for a good four minutes. He had come to refill the surplus gas containers for the generators. He felt a bad craving but knew he'd be on the mountain by himself and feared the hell he would conjure up and decided to be careful. Whiskey was his shaman drug of choice and he knew to avoid spirits.

He left the medicine aisle and got some dried jerky and water instead. He paid the cashier and left. He brought an extra blanket, too, just in case. It was becoming October and he had another month and a half on the mountain. He knew it would start to turn cold soon.

IT WAS 7:00 A.M. and he was working fast; in a couple of hours it would be too hot to work. He was counting the marijuana plants, getting some ready for wet trim, and taking others to the dry room.

He worked up until his midday rest. He sat under a tree and scraped the dirt and THC crystals from his fingertips, "finger hash" as they called it. He would smoke it later.

In his youth, he believed a lot of dumb shit. Like how one time this older fag in the bar relayed to him the origin of "Spanish hash."

"So, in Spain they send young boys running naked through the marijuana fields and then they scrape the THC from their bodies. That's why Spanish hash is so expensive!"

This myth was soon debunked by a fellow weed trimmer.

"Naw, brother," said Austin, this California hippie boy he sat next to in the trim room. "No naked boys, they make that shit from explosives. Butane."

The midday heat was fading and he was back in the garden making sure the plants hadn't changed sex. He started to separate the good pot that would be trimmed and sold as flower from the lesser grade pot that they would consolidate and turn into hash.

Soon the chores were done and he sat drinking water under the shade of a tree. His thoughts always doubled down on themselves at this point in the day. Whenever catching a moment's breath, he had the same feelings. All he could think about was where he had gone.

The last thing he remembered was forgetting all of his lines. It was relayed to him that there were no curse words or jittery, unexpected behavior. Rather, it was a cool and complete disassociation onstage. He went to a table upstage right and buried his face in his hands for a full fifteen minutes. The forty-nine people in the audience got frustrated and eventually walked out. It was his onstage retirement party. That had been some seven years ago. Since then he just chased the fall harvest and did the summer setup for whatever pot farm up north was hiring. He remembered back to earlier in the summer, the day he came to the farm.

Just to be a troll he signed up for one of those Christian free-ride groups, and it had totally backfired. The Christian man he had hitched a ride with was on his way to Oregon from Texas; he made it a point to pray every time they stopped to get gas or take a piss. On one prayer stop, the Holy Ghost spirit lasted for twenty minutes and ended in the Christian man going into full-on testimony. He sat in the passenger seat listening to the man and wished to God (ironically enough) that he could find a ride group where all he had to do was flash his dick and get to his destination in a timely manner. *Next time*, he thought.

The car finally made its way to Lake County. The farm was near there.

Supposedly Clear Lake was the largest lake in California, and supposedly it was the oldest lake in North America. He was told these things but never bothered to confirm them himself.

The car maneuvered around the two-lane highway that circled the lake for miles and miles.

Post–World War II the lake had been a popular Northern California tourist destination; he spied from the car window all the dilapidated fishing piers and run-down motor lodges with the original decaying midcentury signs more or less intact.

The lake itself was fishable, yet the catch was inedible. The mine nearby had closed in the fifties, but not before it had polluted the entire body of water with mercury. It was pure poison.

The car dropped him off at the gas station nearest to the farm and he waited for the farm owner to pick him up. It had once been owned by this dyke who then sold it to a Puerto Rican man from New Jersey.

He watched the new owner pull up to the gas station in a huge black pickup truck, introduced himself, and got in. The owner gave him the rundown—there were ninety-two outdoor plants tucked out past the valley that he would attend to and dry before the seasonal trimmers would come in and manicure the buds. The new owner would fly out every two weeks and give him a ride to the general store to replenish his supplies: drinking water, gas for the generators, toilet paper, and all that stuff. The owner gave him two guns to keep in case Feds or thieves came lurking, and left him on the property to his work.

That was in late July. It was now mid-November. The harvest was over and it was time to return to the city to pay rent and nestle in for the wet, rainy winter ahead.

He sat at the bus stop waiting for his Greyhound to arrive. He decided the bus trip would be nice and didn't want to risk getting another religious fanatic as a driver.

It was raining and he was wrapped in a poncho and had his gear covered in plastic. The line for the bus was full. The unfortunate farmhands who had not shown up early enough to stand under the shoddy bus stop were all standing in the rain.

He looked over to the side and on the ground between the glass screen of the bus stop and the little bench inside sat a full ziplock bag of weed. Someone had either dropped it or left it and he shrugged his shoulders. He actually hated marijuana at this point.

The bus rolled up and all the wet, weary farmers boarded.

He was always taken aback by the beautiful landscape of the area and also by the cultural disconnect of the California backwoods. It was somehow still redneck as all hell—he even saw Confederate flags on bumper stickers here and there. He remembered that an hour outside any city it was business as usual in America.

Later rather than sooner, he arrived in Oakland. He wanted no more of the bus and got off and called a car to S.F.

His apartment was as he left it, sparsely furnished and clean. His life as a farmer had made him want to be a nomad. Every time he came from the mountain he got rid of more and more things. He wanted to be a part-time resident in everything.

For the first time in a long time (and particularly out of nowhere) he felt it, a very strange and foreign emotion; a stillness and a sense of peace. He began to cry. Had this feeling been hiding there, somewhere, all along?

He showered, put on warm sweats, turned on the heater, and began to boil a pot of water for tea. He finally listened to the voicemails on his phone that he had been ignoring all along on the mountain. It was the usual. One from Mark saying how he no longer was hanging out with the blond or the kid with the birthmark, messages from bill collectors, student debt people, his mother (over and over and over again), and one of note.

"Hello, this is Shelia Waters from the Stein Agency in Los Angeles. This message is for Antonio Johnson. We have an offer for you—the role of Jonathan is being revamped for an upcoming movie project based on your old network show *Missed Connections*. We hope this is still your number! We have a *very handsome* offer for you! You can reach me at 310-555-7762—extension 312. Hope to talk soon!"

He had all but stopped breathing. The news hit him in the gut, hard. The show was making a comeback. But, why? It seemed like a thought worth entertaining, certainly. He felt the butterflies in his stomach. He paced for a bit, and thought about a new gym routine, a new diet, going back to his acting coach, finding a place in L.A. to stay for the shooting, but then the kettle began to whistle and he was pulled back into his mind and his apartment.

He poured the hot water on the peppermint tea bag inside the cup and brought it to his bed. He sat down, and, even though it was raining, he lifted up his sweats to his knees and placed his feet out of the window. As quickly as it had rushed through him, his excitement had now left. He tuned out and heard the cars by the highway again. He heard waves. He was back at peace.

He would rest all night and he would not be calling Ms. Waters back, and he would not be doing the movie. He had decided, finally, that he was retired.

ACT III

NO NEW
BOYFRIENDS

MANIFESTO:
NO NEW BOYFRIENDS

ME AND ALL THE REST OF THE BOYS on the block had adopted a very trash-and-burn style with sex: no guilt, no morals, no new boyfriends. It was the rule.

Every once in a while some random two would pair up and monogamy about it. The rest of us talked shit: "Not cool, not anarchist—hoarding all that dick like that. Sexual cap!" (We said shit like this.)

Sometimes the need for something new would pinch me in the ass. Some young thing I was dating would seem like a good idea and I could go wander off in bliss with him for a while. But under no circumstances could he meet my slutty best friends—they would all fuck his brains out, for sure. I would look at the little chicken and think, *The second I wife him he's gonna fuck all my friends*, or, *Actually he's probably already fucked all my friends*, or, the even more precise realization of, *Wait—I'VE FUCKED ALL MY FRIENDS*.

(I wanted to go bathe in penicillin.)

It was a peculiar coven and we kept the circle open. I had many "brothers"; I often called on Nathan on nights when I couldn't scratch my own itch. Nathan lived next door. I had fucked him for five years. His name was Nathan Alexander Carmichael. He was a white boy (hence the name Nathan Alexander).

We had fucked each other so much that sex at times felt like we were scraping the last bit of toothpaste out of a tube that shot its last load two paychecks ago. We had to reinvent our fuck-buddy-hood. The world moved goddamn fast—it was all bills, heartache, and defeat. Those moments of tenderness sometimes had to be engineered.

We did terrible things to each other. It was exciting.

It was his turn to top. He made all the rules for the session. We sat on a clean white bedsheet, naked in his room and across from each other. We were only allowed to talk through text messages. He texted, "Let's pretend we're boyfriends and make love."

"Ok," I texted back. He moved to my side of the bed, and I got a text: "You're not allowed to speak. Lay on the floor." He bound my hands and feet together with suspension ropes and blindfolded me. He left the room and I heard him set something on the floor. I heard him rubbing his hands together and he put something under my nose. "Smell," he said out loud. It was basil. He had to have seen me smile. He put another object to my nose—it was a cloth of some sort with Terre d'Hermès on it, his favorite cologne. I couldn't feel my body anymore. "Open your mouth," he said. I did and he put a piece of cake in it. He rolled me on my back and undid the ropes on my ankles. He pulled my legs up and wrapped them around his hips and entered me. "I own you," he whispered. He forced a pillow on my face and began to fuck me with force. Within a minute he was done, and he put a blanket over me and lay on top. He rubbed my lips with his fingers and kissed me gently. He lifted up the side of my blindfold and exposed my left eye. I saw him wink at me. I was freed.

I put my clothes on and walked out the door and turned to see him standing in the doorway waving at me. I looked at him and saw the same thing I saw when I looked at my right hand: a lifeline, running strong and clear through the center.

MOONLIGHT TOPS
AND THE COLD WAR

THE CITY WAS A GODDAMN TUNDRA. The emotional heat index was, like, negative fifty-three and dropping (and this is summer, mind you).

We were in the middle of a Cold War. I felt like a troop behind enemy lines with no possible chance of escape. It was a suicide mission.

I had fucked some other dude's boyfriend, over and over again, and then a couple more times after that.

His name was Hercules and every other boy in town had fucked him too . . . or so they said. I couldn't confirm it, but

I was at the STD clinic with two other boys who lived on my street so I knew I was at least the third on the block.

"Hercules?" I asked Matty (who lived across the alley).

"Hercules!" He winked when he said it.

I wanted to get swept up in hot memories but my pee hole and pussy were burning and for whatever fucking reason they were playing that "I see dead people" movie.

I could say I deserve better than this—but do I? Really?

"Why do you think you're here?" asked the doctor.

"I get fucked a lot, Doc," I said. "Like, SO MUCH— figuratively speaking I don't have a mother, a last name, or a goal or purpose in life. I'm just a hole." I stopped just short of saying, "My only desire is to be desired. I feel like the whole equation cancels itself out and what it really means is I have no will—I can (at will) rip out all sense of self just so a boy can have one more hole to fuck me in. I'm afraid of this terrible power I wield, I just wait to be wanted, it's killing me, Doctor . . ."

"You'll be fine," said the doctor, writing the prescription for antibiotics and not making eye contact. "I see your kind all the time . . ." He winked at me as he handed me my script.

Matty from across the alley and I took our pills and went for ice cream. We compared notes on the carnage Hercules inflicted. As it turns out we had mutual infections in our butts and not our pee holes, leaving Matty to declare the only strategy we had left in this epic ongoing battle.

"We moonlight as tops and fight the Cold War," he insisted; he was an optimist, a real turn-shit-into-sugar kind of queen.

All I could think about were the gallons of antibiotics that I had poured into my system over the some double-digit number of years I'd been sexually active. I'm sure I'm going to have some form of nerve damage when I'm older (or fucking something)—and so in an effort to thwart all shitty hypothetical scenarios in which I failed, I nervously put on facial moisturizer (at the table at the ice-cream parlor, mind you) and stayed very, very quiet. It's one method of many I use.

Now back to Hercules.

That first time, his boyfriend and I had a three-way. When his boyfriend left for work in the morning, Hercules kept cornering me and shit, and biting me, like SO HARD, to the point that I didn't like it and I said, "We need a safe word."

He looked me square in the eye and said, "Why?" like he was daring me—and that's when I said to myself, *Yes. He gets it.* But that was the first time. I remembered bits and pieces, but the sixth and seventh times were a blur for sure . . . fuck.

Matty bought more vegan double chocolate chip peanut butter cookie dough ice cream. "This will help with the Cold War," he explained, as he heaped another scoop into my already empty plastic container.

Matty left to go be a top, and I was left with the task of putting together a composite of this whole mess with Hercules.

· · ·

I HAD ASKED HERCULES FOR NOTHING, and got more than I bargained for. If I had to think about it I had "won." It was those nights I would come home late and he would be waiting for me at the end of my block. "You free? Can I come in?" he would ask, already knowing what the answer was. I knew the question was a demand, to be honest, but also the more often these nights happened, the more I knew that I had him in my pocket—for whatever it was worth.

Hercules was not particularly handsome, he wasn't particularly hung. The only reason for his extended residency in my psyche was that when he came to consume me, he did it the right way—I literally felt like he might eat me alive.

In the morning, I would awake feeling neutral—not that left-for-dead feeling the other boys on the block stuck me with. I couldn't explain the alchemy that had made me a perfect victim for him, but here I was and here I would stay for a bit.

However wrong his reckless consumption of me was, it mostly felt like a fellow winter soldier handing me a blanket. I was too cold to say no.

I stayed in the ice-cream shop until my vegan double chocolate chip peanut butter cookie dough had melted. My butthole was on fire but I figured I would take a stroll down the block—in for a penny, in for a pound, they say. I would see if Hercules was waiting. If so I would be his snack tonight and take my antibiotics again tomorrow. I would keep trudging this way until the War was over.

REPEATER

HE SAID HE LOST HIS VIRGINITY when he was twelve to his older cousin, who was seventeen. It was on some beach off the coast of Portugal one summer.

"First time, eh? Did you give him poop-dick?" I asked.

"No, man—it was summer, my diet was all oysters and champagne!" He giggled as he pulled my body closer to him.

We were lying naked in bed together, and it was cold outside. It was early spring in Berkeley and the window facing the bay was open. The air was brisk and chilly, but also fresh and sobering. I could see the fog rolling over the streetlights and the orange glow refracting off the fog. It gave that muted orange Creamsicle color I always found peculiar. I missed it whenever I left the bay.

It was chilly but when he said the words "Portugal," "beach," and "summer" I could feel the slap of hot heat on my face and saw blue sky for miles and miles. He always took me there.

"Did we really just have sex?" I asked.

"No!" he said, and looked me in the eye, stern and annoyed, and I already knew what it meant.

This meant, "My boyfriend can't find out." This meant, "This is our secret." To me this meant, "You are somehow disposable."

I got quiet and he noticed. "Stay here a second," he said, and left the bed and went to the bathroom. I lay there in the bed and felt . . . silent.

I looked at the décor of his room. It was very calculated, a mix of midcentury and Northern California rustic. It was all wood, and glass mason jars, and sensible lighting. He had graduated from UC Berkeley, top of his class. He had some tech consulting job in the city and he owned his home. He was only a year older than me. I always felt like I had to be well-behaved, like I was this baby doll thing he would play with until he got tired. He was generous most of the time, though stern at points, but never unkind. He'd bake me things, tell me how "cool" I was, and invited me over every night whenever his boyfriend was out of town. Heaven help me I was defenseless.

I heard the bathtub running. It was his ritual. He always

made me fancy baths, and they were always made of different things. The first time it was five other naked boys and me on drugs dancing around his fireplace. He took me and his boyfriend aside and brought us to the bathroom. "I made this for you guys," he said. It was a warm bath with rosemary, slices of lemon, clover oil, and some herb I didn't recognize. His boyfriend and I sat in the water drinking whiskey. He washed us with soap and poured water over our heads.

This particular bath was lavender, Dead Sea salt, and basil.

"Sit and talk to me," he said.

It was always the same conversation when we were alone. We talked about the first time we met, though neither one of us could really pinpoint it. He was one of those types of friends that you forget exactly how you met them; it's as if they've always just been there. Every year our mutual orbit got closer, then farther, then closer again. Perhaps it started as a chance meeting at an art opening or at a bar but then it inevitably crescendoed into that first night we went home drunk together. Then it would happen again, and again, until it became a pattern.

I sat in the bathtub sideways with my feet dangling out, facing him. He was sitting on the bathroom floor, naked, smoking a cigarette. I hated the way he smoked in the house.

"The problem with you is . . . ," he began, and I winced because that is a horrible fucking way to start a sentence.

". . . that if you really thought about it, you already have everything you need from me," he concluded, sucking on his cigarette hard, like it was a joint or something.

"I've only ever wanted you to acknowledge me," I said.

"You're not my boyfriend. Thomas is," he said, his voice raising a decibel louder, as I expected it would.

He stood up in an angry manner and got in the tub with me. He sat behind me and pulled my body from sideways to lengthwise with the tub. He held me from behind, my head fell on his chest. He dripped single droplets of water on my head from the warm bath; the drops slid off his fingertips to the middle of my forehead. He is the only man who makes me feel this special.

"I've never really asked you for anything," I said, quite meaning it, as I raised my head off his chest to look him in the eye.

"Be quiet," he said, taking my head and gently pushing it back to his chest.

We stayed in the bathtub silent until the water turned cold.

We dried and retreated to bed, wrapped our naked bodies into each other on clean white sheets. I could feel his stomach press into mine and start to sweat before I fell asleep.

Around 3:00 a.m. we were both awakened by his phone ringing. It was his boyfriend, Thomas—he was having some form of crisis. He hung up the phone, his face red and in a panic.

"Hey, let me call you a car home. Thomas is coming over, it's serious," he said in a rush.

"It's fine, I'll walk," I said, already out of bed and putting on my underwear. I got dressed faster than I realized. He kissed me and told me to call him later that day. I heard right through him.

The fog was gone and the night sky was clear, save the orange glare of the streetlight pollution. There was no longer that dreamy orange Creamsicle color, but literally just orange light; it was ugly as hell.

I took a bit of bourbon from my backpack and put on my headphones and decided to drink and meander home the long way. I was not hurt, distressed, or even bothered, only filled with a weird feeling that was somewhere between a premonition and déjà vu, like this was a day that had happened many times before and would also, one day, repeat itself.

MOUNTAIN BOYS

THE SILENCE IS DEAFENING, but that's not the only cliché in the room. There is also the subplot of the playboy and his prey.

I look at my lover and find he is looking directly at me. I am splayed in his DNA and panting hard, and a bit taken aback by what just happened, as my intention was to come over and cuss his triflin' ass out and say I was not going to see him again. Nine months before, I had helped him move into this apartment—all that heavy-ass shit: couch, sofa, appliances, and the bed. The bed was the cruel part. He had said, "Me and you are gonna be spending a lot of time in this apartment together," and then he stopped returning my calls.

Soon after that the pictures started appearing of him and this boy together; they went everywhere, clearly this was his boyfriend. Like, why didn't he make his bitch help him move? I understand that life is by design a competition—okay, this other bitch won, that's fine. But it was twisting the knife to make a boy who you are leading on carry the bed you and your boyfriend are going to fuck on every night. It was this act of hubris, this Agamemnon dancing on the red carpet moment, that made my hatred real.

Now he is smiling deeply at me. I want to smash his pretty fucking face into a car hood.

But then it happens, that moment where all the hate evaporates and it just feels good to see him again, smell him again, feel the weight of him on top of me. He fucks good. Is that all he's good for? In this instant the answer is yes. Our first date had been a year ago—he had ignored me online for a year before that until a mutual friend of ours (who we were both fucking) gave him a solid recommendation for my skills for taking dick. ("He can really take some dick," said the mutual friend to him.)

We sat in bed, postsex sweaty, the first day we met. He said to me, "I'm from the mountains," and picked up a globe off his bookshelf and spun it and pointed to where. "The Andes," he said.

"I'm from the mountains, too." I took the globe from his hands, gave it a spin also, stopped it with my index finger, and pointed. "I'm from the Appalachians," I offered. He smiled at me. "Awww, we're both mountain boys. Cute."

"I grew up surrounded by coffee trees. You?" he asked.

"I grew up in a cotton field—lots of roaches and rats. It was gross," I shot back. He started giggling and eventually we fucked again and again and again until I was convinced that he liked me and that I wanted him. I let him charm me more, I let him let me think I was special—I knew at my core that he was waiting to unzip his face. I'm blindsided by how abruptly it all happened, how fast he left his phone off the hook.

I look at him now and actually laugh to myself. My horrible taste in men is fucking hilarious to me. I blurt it out. "Why didn't you call me back?" I'm grossed out by myself before the sentence fully leaves my mouth.

He answers, "I just wasn't feeling it," and I get that feeling of wanting to break him again.

"Y'know, I know what it's like. I've been in your shoes, too," he adds nonchalantly, making hand gestures and looking to the ceiling. He starts talking, and I zone out. His level of compassion (or seeming lack thereof) is killing me. The emotional distance between us is as wide as the distance between the respective mountain ranges we grew up in—or maybe, even, much, much further. He begins to talk about some boy he fucked before me, someone who refused him, but I guess he can now forgive this person because he's passing the rejection my way. He keeps talking and I tune in just in time to hear him say, ". . . and everybody is left with the ghost of somebody else, aren't they?" I stop to ponder this. If this is true, then there have to be one hundred ghosts in this room already and that's just the baggage I'm carrying. Lover boy for sure has twice as many. I imagine one hundred ghosts in the room (and one hundred only—I don't give a fuck about *his* ghosts). There are too many men here and it doesn't feel like a sexy gang bang. No, this feels like something that's a lot more fucking annoying.

"One hundred boyfriends," I say, deep in thought.

"What did you just say?" he asks, looking at me like he has just been rudely interrupted.

"I didn't say anything," I whisper, as I roll over and turn my back to him.

I begin trying to move past petty emotions and think about this scientifically.

What are the mechanics of desire? In what feels like all of three seconds my mind spins into a hard flashback on past lives—men I loved, some who I eventually hated; they are all still there somewhere, all hovering around. I called them "boyfriends," though this was not always the case. But they were all like pieces of bubblegum you chew hours after the flavor leaves and that you accidentally swallow, and then (supposedly) sit in your guts for seven years. It was like the woman in the eighties who always swallowed her chewing gum and one day the doctors had to surgically remove the tennis ball–sized wad of gum from her intestines—this was the level of exorcism I needed.

I look at the picture of his boyfriend on the nightstand. He is young. He looks very studious. He looks like a young Black man who respects himself. I love him for that because I personally couldn't be bothered with all that at his age. He also looks innocent in a way; perhaps the right word is fragile. I myself am lots of things—petty, jealous, a danger if provoked, certainly sensitive—but not fragile. I could fuck a crocodile and I could survive an atom bomb. This boy who I'm looking at in the picture—not so much. He looks like a child, like he needs a blanket. It's as if he picked this kind of boy just to corrupt him—was that the game? I can tell that this boy doesn't have a clue about the level of whore his boyfriend is. I was called here because this man is bored. Some part of him after nine months is bored with fucking this fragile boy.

My sixth sense tells me that there are aspects of the truth his boyfriend would shit himself over if he knew. This child has probably never seen his boyfriend high on drugs getting fucked by five guys—but I have. What sides of himself does he show this boy that he refuses to show me? I banish the thought as soon as it pops up. I'm sure it would not help me to know, and I want out of here.

I look at the cheater boy and he is snorting lines of cocaine off a hand mirror and watching Black and Latino-themed porn on his computer. He has a hard-on and he looks over at me like it's time for me to bend over again. I sigh internally and feel something that might be like self-esteem—but probably should be more accurately categorized as wisdom—well up in my bones. I've answered every question I needed to hear.

His boyfriend comes in from work early—he failed to tell me that, of course, and I can hear the lock of the front door jostling. I'm beginning to think he did this on purpose; he wants to let his two puppies sniff at each other. I'm feeling violence in me again, but I'm vulnerable because I'm still naked on the bed and feel no great desire to get dressed in a hurry.

His boyfriend walks through the door and sees the lines of coke on the mirror, the porn on the computer screen, and his boyfriend and me naked. He rolls his eyes in this manner that lets me know he has walked into this scene before. Perhaps this boy is not as fragile as I thought. He gets undressed by the bed and says to me, "I need you to sleep on the couch"—I pause for a second and remember that *I* was the one who helped bring the couch in, too. I had some form of sympathy at first but now realize that I don't like my "lover's" boyfriend and that I also can't stand him. Knowing is always half the battle.

I get dressed and, in hating neither the player nor the game, I let my checkered-print Vans pitter-patter softly toward his door. "It's ok, young man, he's all yours," I say, passing the boy.

There is secret sanctimony in me as I close the door and walk away. I would be lying to myself if I believed for a second that I wasn't going to fuck him ever again; I would, for sure. But this next time, my role would be clearer. I would be the ghost who haunted his sex, not the one who haunted his heart.

BOYFRIEND #100 / THE AGENT

NEW YORK CITY WAS BIG FOR NO REAL REASON, much like the mood I was in. He asked me (but really he was *telling* me), "Your writing is great—do you want to be famous?" I was young at the time and believed anything an older, handsome man told me.

"Yes, I want to be famous, it's all I've ever wanted," I said, stumbling naked around his Hell's Kitchen loft, high on Percocet and with nine glasses too many of white wine in my belly. It was the way he always grabbed my chin softly when he really wanted me to hear something he was saying, or maybe the way, on the third night I stayed over, he gave me keys to the apartment.

"The new poems—what's the journey?" he asked. (I hated when agents said the word "journey." No, literally, like, barf.)

"I don't care for a journey," I explained. "I'm just making a map, something that says, 'You are HERE.'"

His eyes always lit up whenever I explained myself. He was older, Jewish, with a body sculpted from some Chelsea gym and I could not *not* want him. He had been a B-boy dancer in the eighties; he showed me the black-and-white pictures of him popping and locking on cardboard on some random sidewalk, proof he had been handsome all his life. I stumbled to his bathroom, a forgotten boom bap soundtrack from some rapper he once fucked blasting in the background on his record player. I closed the door and raided his bathroom cabinet for pills—I knew he would have some. He bought REAL cocaine, like, the kind that came from teeny tiny jars. I bought speed-laced bullshit from little baggies; the shit he had had me rocking and reeling on some other trip. He knocked on the door because he knew that I knew that he knew what I was doing. "The benzos are on the top shelf, baby, take a few for later."

"Okay, thank you," I said.

"I love you, little boy," he said.

"I love you too," I said.

"The new poems are good—if I make you rich will you take care of me?" he said.

"For the rest of my life," I said.

I took the blue pill.

MEANDERING (PART TWO)

SOMETIMES I LIKE WALKING DOWNTOWN, particularly on those days where I say, "I'm not afraid of the world today. I am a citizen of the world!"

My New York boyfriend reached out earlier that morning and tried to brainwash me into domesticity again. "We can get married and have a house in the Hudson Valley, I'll build a fireplace. Do you like fireplaces?" he texted.

"Naw dude, fuck all that," I texted back, but then sort of regretted it.

I was strolling down the street in the East Bay. It was

seventy-four degrees. It was February. It was Valentine's Day AND Black History Month. I felt sexy.

My friend was having a reading at the bookstore downtown. She had written a new play about a genderqueer railroad operator that was set in 1920s Russia. She and her crew were staging a dramatic reading of the text.

There was loads of time to kill before the reading so I went by a particular building; I wanted to see if it had finally been finished. I first found it two days before Valentine's Day last year, when I was out late and chanced upon Yusuf, an Eritrean guy. Twenty-three? He seemed twenty-three.

He had a deep brown complexion with tones of red in it. He looked beautiful under the streetlight and his afro was impressive. His curls were soft. He lived with his brother, who didn't know he was gay, so he fucked guys in the abandoned house by his apartment building that was being fixed up.

The basement was cemented and exposed to entry by these rectangular openings in the wall where I imagined a door would be one day. I shined the light on my phone in the interior to make sure no one was sleeping in there. I also noticed that the windows were all shaped like Moorish doors and there were exposed, stained-wood beams crossing all over the ceiling— the room was unfinished but already beautiful.

The sex was telepathic—we both knew that I wanted to get fucked.

I braced my hands against the cement wall and breathed him in. His dick was right and exact. It was always a rush doing these things with handsome strangers. It was like a familiar roller-coaster ride and though it was obscured from public view in the undone basement, I could still feel the night air on my skin. Pants and underwear down around my ankles, my back and torso lifted, he raised the back of my shirt and hoodie to get more leverage on me, treating my clothes as if they were the reins of a jockey riding a horse. I played with my nipples.

I slowed for a second, though—my mind kept going back to the exposed, stained-wood beams on the ceiling and I felt worldly and sophisticated. I had never gotten fucked and appreciated architecture at the same time. Before I could get too pleased with myself, he finished in me. He gave that god-awful grunt that men do when they want to say, "Ok, let's stop now."

"You gonna call me again?" I said to fuck with him.

"I'm gonna call you all the time," he said as he hugged me from the back and kissed my ear. I knew it was a total fucking lie, but it was still sweet to hear.

I stood in front of the house now—they hadn't laid a hand on it since, and it was still a hollow shell. I was tempted to explore it but decided to get on to the reading.

SOMETIMES I LIKE WALKING DOWNTOWN. On first Fridays they have the art walk festival. I spent last year avoiding it, but decided that it was sunny and time to go. I started avoiding it after I had a series of panic attacks the year before. The last time, I ate a pot cookie and tried to ride the train to the festival. In my head I couldn't shake the thought of hearing bullets coming from some unknown location and a sniper being the cause. I had been reading the newspaper too much, perhaps, but I couldn't even make it to the train entrance, and took an immediate cab home.

Today my sense of doom was somehow nonexistent. I pranced through the art walk and made it to the play reading. I skipped on picking up whiskey and regretted it halfway through the reading because I was falling asleep, and besides, there was the honest-to-god truth: drama is more dramatic when you're drunk.

Either way, by the time the reading was over it was dark outside but still strangely warm. I walked briskly enough to take off the flannel I was wearing. I was strolling through downtown just long enough until I was walking side by side with a car that had been slowly following me for a block.

The older Latino man within demanded I get in and come to his house. I obliged.

He lived in one of the newer high-rises downtown. The floor plan was so complex that it felt like you were in an endless doom of bad gray carpeting and metal gray doors. Like, if he was a serial killer, there would be no way I could both fight him off and find my way back to the front lobby without his help.

He brought me to what seemed like an unfinished workout room and invited me in, leaving the lights off. There was a window with a bit of the moon shining through, and I could track his movements, so it seemed safe enough.

"Do you like dirty fucking asshole?" he said in this voice that was supposed to be dirty and hot, but dear god—*the question*.

"Um, I mean, like, hmmmm, I like, took a shower today . . . ," I fumbled. I'm not really into scat play but also didn't want to come off as judgmental or like a square. He got the hint.

"It's ok—I'll go rinse . . . Wait here," he said as he left the room.

I sat in the unfinished gym of this yuppie-living complex. I was looking up at the exposed wires from where a light fixture would be and thinking to myself, *I should leave*, but at this point I was feeling too horny to go anywhere. Why couldn't he just fuck in his apartment? Ah, he lives with his boyfriend—or someone. Anytime a grown man can't fuck in his own house there is *always* some kind of backstory. And it's never a really interesting one.

The man came back after about twenty minutes.

"How is your boyfriend?" I asked.

"He's watching TV," he explained, pulling down his shorts.

"Does he want to join in?" I asked, just to fuck with him.

"No, we don't have sex anymore," he said, matter-of-factly.

I fucked him doggy-style because it's the easiest way for two strangers to cum. He was facedown pretending that I was someone else. I was watching him facedown pretending that he was someone else. He was facedown pretending that he was someone else. I was watching him facedown pretending I was someone else.

It was over soon.

He slapped me on the ass as I walked out the door of the weird gym. "You'll find your way out," he said, already walking away. Miraculously I did find my way out without any help— maybe I *could* escape a serial killer.

Before I realized what I was doing, I walked all the way northwest of downtown to go back to the mysterious unfinished building. I wasn't sad, bummed, or even slightly inconvenienced, to be honest, but I did have the urge to remember a day that was before today. I had the urge to think about a time that had felt, for lack of a better term, romantic.

HOOKER BOYS (PART THREE)

I HAD DECIDED TO FUCK A HOOKER that night because I was bored and it seemed like the most morally fatigued thing I could do given my circumstances.

I had not been drinking for some months after a title bout I had with four bouncers at the bar down the street. I had saved a bit of cash and figured I should enjoy some specific form of vice. I still did cocaine, but without alcohol it just felt like a wash, so none of that. I thought about maybe just going to spray-paint something, but that just felt "too free," both spiritually and emotionally. I wanted to engage in commerce and challenge myself and the only thing left was to pay for sex with a hooker. "Sober fun" was damn near an oxymoron but I was going to have it tonight, by god, and how!

I scrolled through the grimy site of all the boys slinging dick for money and I felt like I was at some sort of weird shopping mall. They all had "gay face"—that look of over-enthusiasm, or like they had all been male cheerleaders in high school and it had simply fucked up their lives forever: "READY?! OK!"

This one boy caught my eye and we began a correspondence that ended some half an hour later with me sitting in his living room in a fancy apartment on a not-so-distant side of town. He said his partner was away and I could only imagine that this was the partner's apartment as I was sure his hooker salary wasn't footing the bill here, or at least I highly doubted it.

The guy had not been a male cheerleader, in fact, but had for a number of years worked as a flight attendant. I was trying to fill in all the dots by myself and I assumed his flight attendant job was how he landed whatever partner footed the bill for this house—but again, this was all speculation. Or maybe he was a drug dealer too? I had an older second cousin once removed who was a flight attendant and used it as a cover to smuggle ecstasy across the country. He made a decent living at it, too, apparently before he got caught and went to jail, but that was in the early nineties and I can't imagine with the way security culture runs these days that any of that was still possible. Even so, whenever I see flight attendants I equate them to drug dealers and it is at the very least an entertaining false equivalence.

I had also detected an accent that I couldn't quite figure out.

"I'm Nigerian, but spent half my life in London," he explained. "What part of Africa are you from?" he asked.

"Alabama," I replied. He didn't laugh.

In my head I rolled my eyes the same way I always do when African-born Blacks ask that question—like, how the fuck is that a real question? I had flirted with taking that weird DNA test at some point but then I thought it was silly to spend three hundred bucks just so someone could tell me that I'm from someplace in Africa. I already wore the Mark of Ham, I already knew I was "from" Africa, and besides, I thought spending that money to fuck this guy would get me way closer to my roots than any DNA test—like, for sure.

I guess he could see me thinking all this and took control.

"The clock starts now—what's on the menu, mate?" he exhaled as he walked in the living room and sat a cup of tea in front of me. I was confused. Like, when was he making tea? I didn't notice him boiling water, even.

"Will you hold me while I cry?" I asked, like, completely dead-ass serious.

"Absolutely not," he replied. "Your bum is massive—I'll

start there," he said, and motioned over as if to take off my shirt. I stopped him.

"No, like, can we pretend to be boyfriends while we fuck?" Again, I was serious.

"Suit yourself," he said, and his entire face softened and he began again. "How was your day, my love? I've missed you."

We kissed and I was excited because it felt like something really dirty and desperate was happening.

He led me to the bedroom, which had a sparse feeling to it. There was just a bed and a night table and a massage table. Maybe he lived here by himself and really was a full-time hooker? Like, why would a couple live in such a sparse room?

Either way I was on my back on the bed with him on top of me. He was extremely tall and muscular. His dick was only about a notch above average, but his skin was smooth and I thought about how, in my everyday life, I almost never have sex with (or attract?) anyone this muscular—like, was his physique what I was paying for? No, that couldn't be it.

He was going full force on me and started to sweat, and I was looking at his face and couldn't even feel myself get fucked 'cause my mind sat stuck on everything else. Like how muscular his body was, the horrible drab blue color of the carpet and décor of the room, and the fact that he kept whispering "I love you, boyfriend" in my ear.

It suddenly struck me that I hired this man because I was lonely. I almost began to tear up—not out of sadness but out of complete sensory overload. Also, his dick did not feel "great."

I felt like I was a patient about to undergo surgery, and all I wanted was for it to be over so that I could say I did it.

He faked an orgasm long and deep, and I was flushed with relief. He collapsed on me and was sweaty and breathing hard, and I could feel his heart pounding on my chest. He rolled to the side and I tried to leave the bed but he pulled me by the arm closer to him.

"Where you going mate? Your hour's not over yet"—he was breathing heavily, facedown and into the comforter on the bed. I had never witnessed a person's fake orgasm taking so much out of them.

"You must be an artist," he said. "You seem like an artist."

"I did pay sixty thousand dollars for a theater degree—I don't know if that makes me an artist or not," I blurted out, and for the first time he laughed.

"You're a reasonably handsome guy. Why don't you just save your money and get a real boyfriend?" he inquired, still facedown in the comforter.

I paused at the word "reasonably." I just paid him—would it be too much trouble to get a real fucking compliment out of the guy? Like, *fuck*.

He was beginning to feel like a boyfriend in that he was already annoying the fuck out of me.

"Don't be silly," I said, getting up with force this time. "You are my real boyfriend—can I see you next month?"

He didn't look up, instead throwing me a peace sign.

"Is that a yes or no?" I asked, hoping to God it meant yes.

"I'll be waiting right here, boyfriend," he said, finally looking up with this weird, shit-eating grin. "Here I am, I always am," and he plopped his head back into the comforter.

I finished dressing and walked out his door all the way downtown. I walked from there to the lake, and from the lake I walked home, and once I was home I went right to bed.

MR. RALEIGH VS.
THE GYM

MR. DARYL RALEIGH WAS TAKING A SHOWER at the YMCA gym and lingering in the locker room in the same way he had done for twenty years. He was feeling abandoned by the situation.

He had been to the doctor earlier that day. His doctor wanted to put him on testosterone treatment and explained it was because Mr. Raleigh's body wasn't really making it anymore. "Happens to a lot of us," explained the doctor. Mr. Raleigh refused it at first because he had already been horny and violent most of his life—there was something in the cooling of his hormones that felt . . . nice? That same evening at the gym he was on the elliptical watching commercials playing between news segments. An ad for erectile dysfunction played after an ad for hair implants, followed lastly by an ad for testosterone treatment. The testosterone ad showed a montage of one chubby man struggling at the gym, a man with the same build as the first crying alone on a bench in an empty park, and last, a man binge eating. The ad explained that hormone treatment could cure all these behaviors and Mr. Raleigh felt all but personally attacked. The news segment then began by talking about the current drought. The drought was also having certain social effects.

The drought had killed all the gym cruising, though Mr. Raleigh also remembered other droughts. "The droughts inside," he said, lathering his left armpit.

Droughts were factual and personal. Sun and no rain, scorched earth, and dry sky: whenever the news flashed the word "DROUGHT" every Californian had a civil duty and (as suggested by the news) either showered with a friend, took shorter showers, or perhaps didn't even shower at all. Either way, most of the shower population of the men's locker room seemed absent save for Mr. Raleigh and the five other lurkers he had got sick of boning nearly twenty years ago. He wasn't too alarmed; he had survived these droughts before.

When he looked down at his body he felt like it had abandoned him, too. Where had all the years gone? There were ghosts of other bodies floating in and around him. He was looking down at himself from a vertical vantage point—beer belly, modest cock, beautiful skin . . . it was the beer gut that he was cutting (and his hate handles) that led to this excursion of self-inflicted gym torture. He was depressed; he gained weight. He was older, and it didn't just melt away like it used to, so now he would drag his sore body into a daily psychological battle with the elliptical and treadmills at the gym. An hour prior, he had been pedaling away on the elliptical, making direct eye contact with himself in the mirror on the machine, sweating like a whore in a gym, doing cardio in a fear-based manner. He pictured all the men he'd had over the years and the different phases of his body as if they were both moon cycles. But there were no stark conclusions to be made, really—he could never get any man to act right, even when he had muscles. He thought about how some love burns itself up and how some love freezes to death.

He had been dating two men younger than him. One was Ben, and the other was David.

Whenever he thought of Ben all he saw was a baby boy doll wrapped in cellophane. The boy was a living, breathing My Buddy doll. He had even gone so far as to date himself when he explained the reference to Ben.

"My Buddy was this play doll in the mideighties marketed to little boys—the idea was to teach little boys that it was ok to be nurturing, loving, and that it was only natural to have a friend that you take care of," he explained, wasted one night in bed.

Mr. Raleigh himself had been a bit too old for the dolls but he remembered being fascinated by the commercials. The theme song went: "MY BUDDY, MY BUDDY / WHEREVER I GO, HE GOES / MY BUDDY, MY BUDDY / MY BUDDY AND ME."

It was short-lived and by the nineties all men had completely cut out their hearts and little boys had to be ready to do the same—none of that faggot-ass playing with dolls bullshit.

Mr. Raleigh had somehow managed to keep his heart intact. Wherever Mr. Raleigh went, Ben went. The pair attended art engagements, orgies, and even the bathroom together. Mr. Raleigh had been over the lustful side of sex, the wham-bam of it all and the feverish high pitch that eventually washed over him after the climax. He saw in the young boy a chance to step back, to go to dinner, to be held again.

It worked too well. Eventually the young boy held him very still, until the nights became *too* still, so motionless that Mr. Raleigh relied on old tricks. He saw the slow-motion repulsion in Ben's face when he told him that he was sleeping with David.

He saw the sparkle leave the young boy's eyes. He would pay for that.

David was truly his match, unfortunately. Mr. Raleigh always expected the worst, in himself and in other people. He suspected that David had never loved him—he just needed a sponsor. The second Ben was gone David stopped putting out. He even started to fuck Mr. Raleigh's friends. The older man was so lonely and guilty he let it all happen.

The irritating part was that when he confronted him, David would never admit to his trespasses. The boy was too noble to say, "I'm an asshole. I did these things." That was the shit that bothered the old man. Like how David alluded to always having open dialogue but nonetheless kept deep secrets.

In a broad stroke Mr. Raleigh thought about how the Natives of the continent were conquered not entirely by all-out warfare, but by polite-sounding treaties of peaceful words that sounded nice but were total fucking lies. Polite lies are how men conquer, saying empty things while psychically cutting their opponent's throat through unseen actions. He hated the way David was all polite talk and manners. He didn't understand when Mr. Raleigh was drunk and threw things or when he confronted David about fucking his friends. The boy thought this was "too emotional"; he called it "uncouth," even. There would be no closure or resolve. It would all have to be fine.

Mr. Raleigh noticed that he had been in the shower so long the water had turned cold. This was certainly only making the drought worse.

He did his postgym ritual: drying off, and moisturizing, which was usually followed by deep reflections in the mirror, before escaping into the autumn evening outside.

Mr. Raleigh was bent over and drying his toes in front of his locker when he felt it—a finger on the opening of his anus.

He turned around to see a Black gentleman a bit younger than himself. He looked as if he had had a few more weeks at that gym than Mr. Raleigh did; his face was young but his hair was completely gray and there was a sliver of precum hanging from the head of his dick. He was handsome.

Without talking the two men ducked into a shower stall

together and closed the curtain. Mr. Raleigh bent over and was taken aback by the fact that in twenty years he had never been fucked in a shower at the gym. He remembered that his body still had one valuable gift: it was *available*.

Mr. Raleigh threw himself into the ritual—arching his back and moaning, waiting for the gray-haired gentleman to climax. His body knew this dance well.

"The gray hair is hereditary—I saw you staring at it," said the gentleman as he left the shower stall.

Mr. Raleigh was proud of himself. He still had it after all.

He escaped to the outside of the gym, en route to his car.

"I'm never going back to that horrible fucking place ever again," he said, walking away for what he knew would be a long time.

THE BOYFRIENDS (CONTINUED)

Boyfriend Double Zero / The Space Cadet

I had seen a UFO. I had snorted half of the bag of anonymous drugs I had found at the party the night before and

3 . . .

2 . . .

1 . . .

CONTACT!

The night had blended into intangible traces in a format I couldn't have foreseen with my puny imagination alone. Also, upon thinking about the term "outer space" . . . hmmmm, it just felt like a double negative or something? I then saw the

UFO and shit REALLY hit the fan. I kept hoping a spaceperson would hop out, but, like a fortune cookie (from outer space) spitting out a divine message, the paper spilling out of the craft read, "This is a spaceperson-less automated craft; i.e., we don't fuck with you niggas."

Boyfriend #21 / The Gardener

Perhaps the worst was behind him. The one hundred men he had left behind were still behind him. Those godless bitches were the WORST, seriously. He was getting older, and all the houses on his side of the block were going up for sale. His house had bad plumbing but good vibes. A shining castle. It was the most in danger. Either way, like the person he was he tended to his garden, if only in spirit. He would stare from the sundeck, overly caffeinated and ridden by spirits, and say shit like, "I wish that would grow more" or "I wish that would grow less." (Attempts at control were frequent.) His own personal plumbing was still fucking EXCELLENT. He could rub one out and still shoot clean over his head on a good day just like when he was a teenager. But, of course, like any realest/toughest bitch, he betted all on losing it one day, i.e., the house he was renting and also the super plumbing in his dick, but he chanted to himself on those mornings he would psychically garden: "I must not think bad thoughts . . . I must not think bad thoughts."

Boyfriend *69 / The Telepath

He had been praying for something more angular. A stiffer collar on his polo, or perhaps to psychically know who was calling before the phone was even ringing, but like all Earth dwellers he knew all too well the limitations of gravity. Gravity . . . ugh, he was so fucking over her. But he settled for the small things in life, like how caller ID was as close to telepathy as he was ever going to get. "BUMMER." ☹

Boyfriend #92 / The Psychiatrist

I explained to him that I had always ended up washing my hands longer than I wanted to. I would always get hypnotized by the motion of my hands and the sound of the water running, and my mind would always double back to where I went wrong in life. It would stop somewhere in a black hole and my anxiety wouldn't pull out of it. He said it was all related to me noticing my triggers more (he was a psychiatrist who studied neuropsychological shit). I didn't know how to explain to him that I did not often want to talk to that part of my brain. I didn't say it because it sounded reckless, but I was afraid that if I kept that light on in my brain all I would notice is that I'm mostly triggered all or most of the time. I'm so serious. The train triggers me, the walk to the train, the unwanted eye contact, the way my body behaves when I notice that I'm being noticed. I figure when someone like me is hyper in tune with their trigger light, it's tantamount to a gazelle in the Serengeti—the feeling that

something is always coming to eat you. I'm sure I could separate the part of my brain where awareness equals constant
panic, but naw, I knew myself. I also casually mentioned my
drinking problem and he explained to me that maybe I just
had excellent neurological uptake and I thought how that was
so much sweeter than him saying, "You're a selfish man who
can't change."

DO THEY EXIST IF NO ONE'S WATCHING?

IT'S LIKE MY FAVORITE SAYING, "Where God closes a door, He opens a window," but in this particular case the window was on the fifth floor and the house was on fire.

The man to my right—he looks like he is ready to jump from a burning building.

I sit listening to this awkward couple next to me as I wait for a friend at a Burmese place on Telegraph Avenue. I like listening to other people's conversations the same way I like looking at the text messages of friends who leave their phones unlocked. I lurk so hard I almost get whiplash. I lurk so hard

I should wear a cape and fangs. I lurk so hard . . . you get the picture.

I am often convinced I care more about these conversations than the participants themselves do. In the case of the burning-building-jumper-man next to me, I know for a fact this is true. The man is on a date—a very awkward date—with a boy too young for him. The man looks fifty (or maybe he's just in his thirties and had a hard life?); the younger man looks like he's twelve, but has to be at least twenty-one because he's drinking a mason jar full of some cocktail—he's lit as fuck. He's red in the face and gesticulating through his speech intensely.

My dinner partner is thirty minutes late. I have heard the man say absolutely nothing while the boy stammers on about how his younger brother can't find the right college, in fact RE-FUSES to find the right college, and how it's making the boys' white-ass mom sad—like, suuuuuuuper sad. Like, so sad she got the boy's younger brother a trip to Yosemite for his birthday to clear his head.

The older man looks as if he wishes to God this interaction had just been a blow job, but I can't imagine how one would get a dick in this young man's mouth: he talks too fucking much.

Back when I was a young and easily corruptible homosexual, all the Daddies loved me because I knew how to shut the fuck up and take some dick.

An older guy would take me to dinner and I would study

him like a cat watching an object it was, at any moment, about to pounce on; i.e., "THIS PUSSY KILLS."

I would answer every question but keep content to a minimum. "I'm studying art," I would respond, or, "I graduate the year after next," or "I was quoted by *The New York Times*"—just enough to let them know that they were about to stick their dick in a young man who had self-worth and a locatable dignity, even though I have to say I wasn't altogether interested in it (the dignity, that is).

My good-boy routine was for the Daddy's relief, not mine. I just wanted to get fucked good—winning the older gentleman's respect was for his peace of mind.

And then I would sucker punch him.

Right as dinner was over and he signed the check, I would stretch and yawn and casually say to my host (in one breath), "Y'know, sir, I would let you cum in me."

Now, most of the men would be immediately disgusted. They'd give me a look of disapproval and I would never see them again, but that was well and fine because they were exactly the ones I wanted to weed out.

It was the Daddies whose hearts you could see skip a beat and a look of exactitude would crawl across their faces.

"Really?" they would say, standing up quickly. These Daddies would take me home, bend me in half like a pretzel, fuck me so hard that I would forget the person I was before they fucked me.

But back to the dinner itself. During the dinner, when the Daddy would be sizing me up, I had the dual occupation of being present enough for him to assess, and also being able to sink into the background enough so as not to take up too much space at the table. I had to treat myself like I was something on the menu he had ordered. Like I was on the menu.

And then a joint lit in my head. I was forgetting something. I had to stop all this thinking and go back. *Horny Daddies . . . I'm on the menu . . . Food . . . Where is my food??*

I'm looking at the waitress and she is motioning as if to say, "One second, please," and I look at the couple that I had just ripped apart for no reason and I think I am being this level of bitch 'cause my sugar is dropping.

I don't know why I got so addicted to the narrative of these men. I need not notice them at all.

It's kind of like that tree-falling-in-the-woods question. Do they exist if no one's watching? I think not, yet still, I can't help wanting some kind of restorative justice blow job for the victim of the date, and, truthfully, one for myself.

Earlier that day my newest HIV counselor saw my chart and noticed I had contracted syphilis three times in one year. She was an older gray-haired straight woman—she hugged me and asked, "Have you ever considered having a boyfriend?" I started crying. Like really, really loud, ugly crying. I had to catch my breath at times I was crying-so-hard crying. Not out of sadness, or loneliness, but out of sheer exhaustion. I was just cocaine hungover and cranky, to be honest, but the echo chamber of the STD clinic was feeling like a coffin I had been submerged in, one I kept reemerging from like a tomb. I was my own personal Jesus.

I cried so hard that she referred me to a mental health counselor who then referred me to HR who then informed me that I should have the first counselor fired for triggering me so hard. The thought of swift justice filled me with an immediate sense of purpose that faded in all of ten seconds. One thing I can truly say I love about myself is that I'm too sketch to lead a moral campaign against anybody. Also, leading a moral campaign against anything just seemed like a lot of work and I was stoned.

Still, I remember her hugging me when I was upset and how nice it felt. Like someone actually fucking cared. No one I was fucking cared for me or hugged me, so in the end I really was a hit dog hollering. It all struck a nerve.

The waitress comes back with three different fried items, coconut rice, and a hot tea, and I'm sitting there looking at the color palette of the food and, for what I'm sure are very specific reasons, I'm thinking about that Frida Kahlo painting where she's in a tub and seeing, like, visions of her life or whatever. I'm thinking of this as I see the food but it's not as poetic, beautiful, or elegant as it sounds—in fact, what I see isn't even a vision but rather a scene, jackhammering its way into my brain, one I can see even when my eyes are closed.

I think back to the interaction with the HIV counselor and the linger of the hug, the humanness, the warmth, the depth, and then my mind falls a little further to the smell of the old lady herself, and then kind of wishing she had a dick and had instead been a creepy old doctor dude who tried to finger me.

I know it's a bad thing to think, but it's ok to think it as long as you don't say it out loud, so I keep it to myself and don't blurt out "I AM HAVING A FANTASY ABOUT PAINTING A DIFFERENT GENDER ON MY HIV COUNSELOR AND HAVING THEM SEXUALLY ASSAULT ME" to the people to my right who are having a terrible date.

I also play the scene in my head of me picturing myself as a *for real for real* shady bitch and actually going to HR and trying to explain all of this.

"But if I had to think about it, what's REALLY getting my goat about the situation isn't the fact that the doctor *didn't* finger me, it's more that she *emotionally* fingered me. She *emotionally fingered me* without my consent!"

My dick is hard and I stare around the restaurant.

No one here cares that my dick is hard.

I don't care that my dick is hard.

I'm back to being just stoned and hungry. I go full force into all the food. I'm eating so fast that I can't even really taste what I'm eating, it's literally just sliding down my throat.

The couple next to me grabs the check and leaves, and with no one left to watch I find I have a strange sense of aloneness— the person I'm waiting for is clearly not coming at this point. But I sink inside myself and remember that I am not alone. I am in a restaurant, full of people.

EPILOGUE

ROCK 'N' ROLL IS DEAD TO ME—
A EUROPEAN TOUR DIARY

I SAT THERE IN THE CVS MAGAZINE AISLE shaking and crying, feeling overwhelmed and a bit beside myself. It was as if the entire fucking Earth simultaneously stood still and switched magnetic poles. Normally I only go to CVS to buy lube and taquitos but today was a bit more ceremonious—before me, I was witnessing the impossible: my band was on the cover of *Rolling Stone*. The article had gone as far as to declare me "The Rouge King of California Garage Rock." I, like, gagged. The illuminated neon fluorescent thought bubble above my head was flashing between *The Rouge King of California Garage Rock?! OMG! Girl! Like, THAT'S ME!* and also *I hope this gets me laid.*

I walked home with the magazine in hand and stared at my face again on the cover. I thought about time, placement, and lineage. My very existence in the rock matrix felt something like the past, present, and future all colliding at once. I thought about the day Robert Johnson sold his soul to Satan and the subsequent birth of rock 'n' roll. Did Father Johnson have any clue how many times and how many waves of blues music would be repackaged and sold to the world, over and over and over again? For certain no, but here I was—I was quite possibly the last Black man playing R & B–influenced rock music. I had been to a Black rock festival last summer where the moneyed Blacks mutually congratulated one another for their obsession with anime and all their bands sounded like nineties death metal. No like really, what the actual fuck? As if that weren't all alienating enough, I sat in mute horror as they didn't book my band for yet another year and instead hired a full-blown Caucasian SoundCloud rapper who, in the middle of his set, yelled, "My great-great-great-grandmother was supposedly half-Black and I want to dedicate this performance to our collective struggle as stolen African peoples!" and everyone collectively raised their fists. I immediately left the festival and was ready to admit that these niggas were so literally *not* my crew.

In a world where white rappers were winning and I was decidedly not, I did the only thing a person in my situation can do in America—I fucked a white dude to get ahead.

Carl Mitchens had been the seminal underground rock boy-genius back in the eighties and nineties, and he now signed bands to his uberhip indie-rock label and pipelined them to midlevel commercial success. He was also a known closeted bisexual with a fetish for bottoms who dressed like seventies disco divas. He informed me that his hippie-ass wife and three kids were in Tibet for some invasively white religious celebration thing and I almost barfed but also seized the opportunity. I dressed up like Donna Summer in the "Bad Girls" video, complete with silk stockings and garters and a bob wig, and let him fuck me on his kitchen table. Postcoitus I slipped him my band's demo tape, and six months later we had a magazine cover and a European tour.

Now, if this had been the nineties, a *Rolling Stone* cover would have meant that you could at the very least buy a house in Los Angeles. These days it meant that you could go to Europe (Americans didn't go to rock shows anymore), come home broke, but not starve to death on tour. It seemed like a fair enough trade—my band accepted the challenge.

THE DAY ARRIVES. The drummer, the bass player, this roadie I was in love with, and I meet at the airport, and we are ready to rage. We have a layover in Iceland on the way to our first stop, Amsterdam, where we'll meet our tour manager. Carl had only hired her the day we left because someone else had pulled out last minute. We land in Amsterdam and have three days to kill before the tour starts. We meet the tour manager, a rad German woman who we crashed with. Roadie lover boy and I immediately start fighting and the bass player and drummer go to explore the city. The rock promoter Carl knows is going to meet up with us for stints in the U.K. and also Germany. Amsterdam is a blur of hookers, beer, psychedelics, and anxiousness. What would this tour be like? I end up hooking up with this famous Dutch writer, who says to me, "Well, you're a bit overweight but you have a gorgeous face"—with his dick still in me, no less. I take him to meet up with roadie lover boy and they double penetrate me for all of ten seconds. The next day we go out of town to pick up the tour van, amps, and drums. The tour is underway.

BRUSSELS, BELGIUM—Our first gig is a rock 'n' roll house party in Brussels. The kids are cool and our set is banging. There are no sluts at the show. We go to get a falafel after. Roadie lover boy and I argue but I don't remember what about. The house gives us free beer and makes us pancakes.

ROTTERDAM, NETHERLANDS—This gig is at a big venue and it is some sort of festival with a shit ton of Dutch people dressed like sailors. The Dutch writer comes to see the show. I remember only older women dancing. We stay at a superfancy hotel by the river that looks like a forty-story, lopsided Lego block, stacked recklessly on another. The roadie lover boy is also, as it turns out, a Catholic mystic, and he makes a plan to visit all the oldest cathedrals in every city we go to starting with this one. I go out with roadie lover boy to all the gay bars in Rotterdam—they are obnoxiously clean and it makes me realize that everything in America is really fucking dirty. *I'm* really fucking dirty. We both get picked up by this twenty-two-year-old boy from Martinique—he looks like what would result if roadie lover boy and I had a son. We take turns fucking him until the sun comes up.

ANTWERP, BELGIUM—This show is at a circus-themed bar. Attendance is low and the guy who runs the club explains that the city has been slow after the terrorist attack at the airport. There are girls flirting with the bass player (as always) and after the show we stay at the band apartment upstairs. I am really intrigued by the garage rock kids in Europe. They all dress like stereotypical Californians. It's weird. I think they think that I surf. I find myself explaining that I live in Northern California and the water is always cold there. They are intrigued by the fact that I manicure marijuana for a living. The other band is a two-piece and I think they sound like the Immortal Lee County Killers. I tell them that but they only know garage bands from the present—not seventeen years ago. After the show, I do the purest cocaine I have ever done in my life and I stay up all night with roadie lover boy. He tells me that he loves me.

LONDON, ENGLAND—We take a ferry over to England and it's a shit show. I takes like three hours to get into England, and after what seems like forever customs gives us our passports back and they hand me the bass player's, as if I look like a smaller light-skin Black boy with dreads. I'm already over it. We play a show in Camden Town. Someone tells us that Amy Winehouse lived super close to the venue but I went looking for her old apartment to no avail. I have sex with some random dude before the show at his really tiny apartment. The gig is up a flight of stairs and I'm tempted to quit on the spot—99 percent of rock 'n' roll is carrying amps upstairs and my fat ass is over it. There is a very tall and very handsome Nigerian boy who comes to the show to tell me that he loves my band. He is easily one of the most handsome men I've ever seen. He looks like a young Idris Elba but even more handsome—it's insane. I, like, can't even talk to him. The boy in the band that is opening up for us is bisexual and from Tennessee originally; we make out while his girlfriend isn't looking. We end up staying the night at a friend's mom's house. We leave after roadie lover boy visits a cathedral.

STAFFORD, ENGLAND—We are in the North of England and the place we play was an indie disco at some point in the late seventies and early eighties; I know this because the dad of one of the boys in the opening band told me so. We have a cool set and we sleep at the club. Roadie lover boy and I get drunk and get into a fight again. He leaves the venue to go fuck some leather Daddy.

BRIGHTON, ENGLAND—I love Brighton. I went there on tour for the first time some twelve years before this trip. I meet up with a boy from Bristol who I was once engaged to—we are still in love, we decide. We also finally meet up with our mysterious rock promoter man. He's an Irish-English dude. Handsome bugger. He's based in Berlin but his parents live in Brighton, and we go to his parents' house. We are in Brighton for two days. The promoter's American cousin is there and is making us a macaroni casserole dish. He is booking some other band from Austin, Texas, and we are taken off the bill of the underground queer show to play at a bigger venue with the Texas band. I'm intrigued by the Austin band because they are exactly what I expected, to a T. They are playing bar rock note for note—they are even wearing ponchos and cowboy hats. They are all really sweet guys. The night before, we did cocaine with them and the rock promoter until the drummer put his foot down. He is vegan and straight edge and will have none of these shenanigans anymore. Roadie lover boy goes on a date with an African boy and I go fuck a ginger. After the show, the bass player is mad at me; I make a joke about fucking a skinhead, again. He hates that. I get drunk and leave my guitar at the venue.

LILLE, FRANCE—We get to the ferry early in the morning and sail to France. On the way to the show we buy me a guitar at a music shop and get to the venue. It is a vegan café that has shows in the basement. We sound check and I go to fuck a man I met online in the basement of the restaurant where he is on break. We cannot understand a word the other is saying; we just follow a pin in the app until we see each other, and I think at first, when he is taking me to the basement, that he is leading me to my death. I'm so horny I follow. The show is cool and we party in Lille. Roadie lover boy meets another Black boy, he's DL or something and gets nervous when roadie lover boy takes a picture of him. The Black boy takes the phone but gives it back after a few minutes. We get back to the band flat at five in the morning and the German tour lady is over it. "NO MORE TOMCATTING!" she screams. The van leaves early.

PARIS, FRANCE — Show is canceled.

RENNES, FRANCE — Show is canceled.

SAINT-ÉTIENNE, FRANCE — This place is fucking hilarious. The show is chill and I go home with this gay art student boy, the bass player goes home with gay art boy's straight best girlfriend, roadie lover boy goes and fucks some dudes somewhere, and the drummer and the tour manager stay at the owner of the venue's place. No one tells anyone where they are going. On the way to his house the gay art student boy buys a baguette out of a vending machine and I'm taken aback because it's like, you know, so French. He takes pictures of his dick in me, and punches me in the middle of the night because I am snoring too loud. It's daybreak and I realize I have no clue how to find my bandmates in this confusing city. I go to the venue but the bass player is missing for another two hours. He finally skateboards up and the tour manager cusses all of our triflin' asses out. The drummer and the tour manager relay how fucking weird the owner of the venue was. He is an American from California who has lived in France for twenty or so years. He has a Confederate flag hanging up at his house and when I hear that I giggle. Like, the thought of a guy from California, waving a rebel flag in France of all places. The humor is lost on the others. We quickly get the fuck out of Dodge.

LISBON, PORTUGAL—This place is gorgeous. There is the smell of seafood cooking all over and I can see the ocean from, like, everywhere. The guy who booked our show is a fucking babe—we are playing some form of festival but I can't make out what it is exactly because I don't speak the language. Roadie lover boy and I go to a restaurant and hear fado music and then we go have sex with this really rich guy. I get fucked by him while he's getting fucked by roadie lover boy. We get in trouble with the rest of the crew—in Europe, all the venues provide a meal for the band and it's considered rude not to show up. I apologize to the chef when I get back to the venue. The opening act is a local teenage girl band. They sound strangely jazzy and the singer is dancing like Christina Aguilera. They are really sweet. Later that night on the way to the booker's house he and I make out.

MADRID, SPAIN—The show here is chill. A radiator (or something) explodes in the back room and the tour manager's computer gets wet. Roadie lover boy gets his bag stolen, and I hook up with a man from Shanghai. I do not remember where we stayed.

BARCELONA, SPAIN—Either the show in Barcelona got canceled or we had a true day off, I cannot remember. Either way we all split up. Drummer and bass player go to a hardcore show and the German tour manager lady goes to a friend's house so she can get away from the sausage party that is the tour van. Roadie lover boy and I go wild in Barcelona; we go hunting for bathhouses so we can fuck people all night. We end up at the beach and then the fashion warehouse of some random guy we meet. They take turns fucking me on the couch there; we all wash up in the sink after. We later go to a bar with a back room and roadie lover boy stays and charms everyone in the bar while I go to the back room to fuck. I meet a Colombian man and fuck him and mention to him that my partner (roadie lover boy) is from Colombia, too. We all go back to his house and I am made to wait in the lobby while they fuck upstairs. Roadie lover boy comes down after with a smile on his face. He says he could feel my cum in the man while he was fucking him and that made him feel even closer to me. We kiss. We go to a rave to meet up with some friends from San Francisco who happen to be at a club DJing that night. A huge thirteen-person brawl between security and some club goers erupts outside and we leave en route to a bathhouse. Outside the bathhouse a couple of shady characters are waiting. They come and grab me—not violently but sensually, as if they are flirting. Really, they are stealing my phone from my pocket. Roadie lover boy and I stay in the bathhouse until 8:00 a.m.

LYON, FRANCE—This place is stunning. We play a show on a houseboat and the opening band is killer. The city has steep steps everywhere and a French boy tries to take me away after the show. I decline because roadie lover boy is leaving back to Colombia soon and I want to be with him. We end up staying in Lyon for two days.

TOULOUSE, FRANCE—This show is full of French mod Daddies on vintage Vespas and I literally have a boner the whole time. Roadie lover boy leaves because he has to get back to Colombia; he is staying with extended family in Paris first. We say that we will love each other forever and then kiss goodbye.

MARSEILLE, FRANCE—Show is canceled.

TÜBINGEN, GERMANY—The show here is at a squat called Epplehaus Jugendzentrum. It's punk as fuck. The opening band is three German guys who have this, like, Mexican-themed band. It's so fucking offensive. It's literally them doing a German-sounding Speedy Gonzales impersonation the entire set. I think one of them even puts on a sombrero. The drummer of our band, who is part Mexican, mind you, looks at me as I am looking at him and our jaws both drop. Like, why is this happening? After the show, I get fucked in a bathroom at the squat by a student boy and then I get fucked by a Middle Eastern guy I follow home. The bass player and I find a Slayer sweatshirt at the show and spend the entire rest of the tour fighting over it. The bass player eventually wins.

FREIBURG, GERMANY—I remember passing through the Black Forest in Germany. The tour manager is threatening to stop and do a séance, because the Black Forest is a romantic site of witchcraft in German lore, and I really want to join. All I remember from this show is the DJ playing the Raincoats and me rimming a boy in a bathroom.

PRAGUE, CZECH REPUBLIC—This is the farthest east I've been in my life. I can't get a feel for this city and we are only there for the night. The tour manager is getting hit on by a girl who brags about drinking her period blood for health, and a man shows up who says he's been in love with our band for years. We stay in a hostel that night that is so creepy I can't deal. There is a dead rat in the kitchen but from the looks of it, it seems like the rat wasn't even poisoned—it seems like it had simply just given up on life because this hostel was so bleak. We leave the next day and get stopped by the cops for having Polish license plates.

KASSEL, GERMANY—This town is all rock. I'm excited to see so many people show up. I don't have the slightest fucking clue how they really know about us, but I will take it. The venue owners light a couch on fire outside the venue and the fire department shows up. Besides the couch fire, all I remember after the show is going home with a handsome German writer whose roommate wouldn't stop making out with me. It was fun and the next morning he says to me, "You and me will meet twice in this life," right before I close the door to the tour van.

BERLIN, GERMANY—I basically hate touring. It's all long rides and waiting for hours in clubs. But of course, it also beats staying at home all the time, so nevertheless, I persist. We meet up with our European booker at his flat in Berlin and play the show in a neighborhood called Gesundbrunnen. We wait for hours at the venue, play, and immediately drive fourteen hours back to Amsterdam to catch our flights in time for Dubai.

DUBAI, U.A.E.—So these two rad ladies who throw an indie rock party in Dubai got wind that my band was in Europe and offered to fly us over to Dubai and pay us good and put us up in a luxury hotel for three days with separate rooms. I felt like a member of Mötley Crüe but also was heeding the warnings of all my friends to be really careful in Dubai. We land and take a shuttle to customs and the bass player lets out a fart so far-reaching in its gnar-i-tude that this other woman and I on the shuttle almost hurl and the bass player starts giggling. We are in customs and everyone gets groped and strip-searched except me and I am rather bitter about it. We play at an Irish pub (???) and it's a huge bar. There're so many drunk English people

I'm slightly taken aback by how many British immigrants in Dubai dress like those assholes from *Jersey Shore*—I really, really don't get it. We play the show and I use an amp that was autographed and used for recording by Nile Rodgers. The crowd is wild and I am unlearning all the lies they taught us about the scene here. Everyone's wasted: dykes are making out with each other, and some dude throws up in the fountain outside. This Nigerian bouncer is staring at my ass like he wants to stab it with his dick and I get goose bumps.

The next day we are taken to the souks across the river and it's a shit show. The bass player and I are both wearing dashikis and the Emirati store owners are yelling from their shops, "AH, HAKUNA MATATA!!" and also "HEY, OBAMA!"; not being able to decide if this is racism or an ill attempt at intersectional camaraderie we both just smile. One shop owner grabs me in a headlock and takes me into his store and demands I buy something. I don't know if it is customary to bargain with the shop owners so I just ask the price (willing to pay whatever) and he stares at me cold and says nothing ('cause basically, like every other man in my life, bowing to his word is still getting me nowhere). The party promoters take us out for food and my bass player orders a camel burger—I don't think to ask how it tastes because I don't want to know. The promoters hear that I am from the Deep South (of the United States) and take me to an American restaurant that actually has spot-on soul food. I am shook. The next day we fly back to Amsterdam.

• • •

AMSTERDAM, NETHERLANDS—We were supposed to continue another two weeks in Scandinavia but all the shows fall through. We change our tickets and spend three days in Amsterdam. I go that night to a fetish bar with a piss-play area in the back and bunks for fucking. An older Iranian man strips me naked and ties me to a bunker pole and binds my wrists and ankles together. He lays me on my side in the bunkers and takes off his belt and whips me hard across my bare ass while he is fucking my mouth. He climaxes over my face and unties me and begs to meet me again and I giggle. I go home with a Dutch man who explains he is suffering from depression. I leave his home in the morning and spend literally two days in the bathhouse downtown. Eventually we fly home to San Francisco and we are all completely broke.

ACKNOWLEDGMENTS

I would like to thank my mother, Annie Jewel, for passing the gift of the pen; my sister, Danielle, for being my fiercest protector; and my nephews for reminding me that my job as an older brother will never be done. I would like to thank my wife, Sophia Wang, for the years of limitless support and guidance. Special thanks to my special friend Ryanaustin Dennis for showing me how all love can work. Thank you to my bandmates, Sean Teves and Ezra Rabin (the Younger Lovers). Kenyon Farrow for being a constant ear to listen and shoulder to cry on. Michelle Tea for mentorship, guidance, and really believing in me. Channing Joseph for my hilariously tumultuous time at *SF Weekly* (lol). Justin Torres for reading my first zine, *Fag School*, and saying to me, "You have a spark." Mike Albo for letting me fanboy this long. Kathleen Hanna for the years of patience, support, and inspiration. And Janelle Hessig for dragging me on tour and always being down for a road trip.

To all my New York City Brother Lovers: Zac Ching, David DeWitt, Adam Rhodes, Adam Baran, and Nicholas Teixeira. To all my Los Angeles Brother Lovers: Darren Kinoshita, Seth Bogart, Eric Shum, Mike Hoffman, Jack Shamama, and Bradford Nordeen. To all my San Francisco / Oakland Brother Lovers: Gary Gregorson, Jesse Carlo Parsons, Zac Benfield, Sean Dickerson, Ethan Mitchell, and Ben Brown. Shout-out to the special women in my life: Schentell Nunn, Xandra Ibarra, Paulina Lara, and Kenya Robinson.

I would also like to thank the UC Berkeley MFA Art Practice department. (GO BEARS!) Faris Al-Shathir for giving me the opportunity to finish the first pass at *100 Boyfriends* as part of the BOFFO artist residency on Fire Island. Jennifer Baumgardner of Dottir Press for taking a chance on me and publishing my children's book. Bob Burnside for being a magical wizard mentor. Malcom Gregory Scott for being a magical wizard mentor.

I want to extend loads of love to everyone at MCD / Farrar, Straus and Giroux for rocking with this joint. Also a special thanks to everyone at the Whiting Foundation—what a difference an award makes! Thanks to Jamia Wilson and Jisu Kim at the Feminist Press (my alma mater). A super deep and special thanks to Julia Masnik—my formidable agent and rad mom, who took a chance on me. A special thanks to all my ex-boyfriends and future ex-boyfriends—may our love rest in peace. And last (but never least), my editor and beautiful friend Jackson Howard for helping me conjure up the Devil with this book.